Praise for *Cupid, Inc.*

"*Wow* . . . this is an erotic romance that truly hits the mark. There are great, detailed scenes that leave you panting for more."
—The Romance Reader's Connection

"A top-notch quartet of tales that are guaranteed to singe your fingers. . . . What an enjoyable way to get revved up for Valentine's Day . . . spending it reading *Cupid, Inc.*" —Romance Reviews Today

"I love Michele Bardsley's *Cupid, Inc.*! It's sexy and erotic, and the humor will make you grin at the same time you're squirming in your seat."
—Cheyenne McCray, author of *Forbidden Magic*

"[Bardsley's] understanding of people's need to love and be loved is uncanny, [so] it is no small wonder that *Cupid, Inc.* is such a wonderful read. . . . Bardsley has a wonderful knack for writing a page-turner that is not only enjoyable but also witty and full of good humor . . . a wonderful book!"—Roundtable Reviews

"I enjoyed each and every one of these stories. I love stories with . . . gods and goddesses in them, and this collection is one of the best!" —The Best Reviews

"Funny and sexy stories. . . . [It is] evident that one of the author's trademarks is to put so much humor into hot and sexually charged stories. Readers will laugh out loud many times, and they will be searching for ice and fans or their partner to cool the flames this book will stir up." —Love Romances

"Lively, sexy, out of this world . . . fun! Michele Bardsley's vampire stories rock!"
—Carly Phillips, *New York Times* bestselling author

Praise for *Don't Talk Back to Your Vampire*

"Utterly fun and witty." —Gena Showalter

"Cutting-edge humor and a raw, seductive hero make *Don't Talk Back to Your Vampire* a yummylicious treat!"
—Dakota Cassidy, author of
The Accidental Werewolf

"A fabulous combination of vampire lore, parental angst, romance, and mystery. I loved this book!"
—Jackie Kessler, author of *The Road to Hell*

"All I can say is *wow*! I was totally immersed in this story." —The Best Reviews

"A winning follow-up to *I'm the Vampire, That's Why* filled with humor, supernatural romance, and truly evil villains." —*Booklist*

Praise for *I'm the Vampire, That's Why*

"From the first sentence, Michele grabbed me and didn't let me go! A vampire mom? PTA meetings? A sulky teenager? Throw in a gorgeous, ridiculously hot hero and you've got the paranormal romance of the year. Get this one *now*." —MaryJanice Davidson

"Hot, hilarious, one helluva ride. . . . Michele Bardsley weaves a sexily delicious tale spun from the heart." —L. A. Banks

"A fun, fun read!" —Rosemary Laurey

continued . . .

Because Your
Vampire Said So

Michele Bardsley

A SIGNET ECLIPSE BOOK

SIGNET ECLIPSE
Published by New American Library, a division of
Penguin Group (USA) Inc., 375 Hudson Street,
New York, New York 10014, USA
Penguin Group (Canada), 90 Eglinton Avenue East, Suite 700, Toronto,
Ontario M4P 2Y3, Canada (a division of Pearson Penguin Canada Inc.)
Penguin Books Ltd., 80 Strand, London WC2R 0RL, England
Penguin Ireland, 25 St. Stephen's Green, Dublin 2,
Ireland (a division of Penguin Books Ltd.)
Penguin Group (Australia), 250 Camberwell Road, Camberwell, Victoria 3124,
Australia (a division of Pearson Australia Group Pty. Ltd.)
Penguin Books India Pvt. Ltd., 11 Community Centre, Panchsheel Park,
New Delhi - 110 017, India
Penguin Group (NZ), 67 Apollo Drive, Rosedale, North Shore 0632,
New Zealand (a division of Pearson New Zealand Ltd.)
Penguin Books (South Africa) (Pty.) Ltd., 24 Sturdee Avenue,
Rosebank, Johannesburg 2196, South Africa

Penguin Books Ltd., Registered Offices:
80 Strand, London WC2R 0RL, England

First published by Signet Eclipse, an imprint of New American Library,
a division of Penguin Group (USA) Inc.

First Printing, May 2008
10 9 8 7 6 5 4 3 2 1

I adore MaryJanice Davidson, who is honest, sarcastic, supportive, weird, and disgustingly talented. She never forgets to tell me to drop dead. Now, that's love, people.

To my sister, Candy
You haven't killed anyone or gone stark
raving mad. That's really damned amazing.
I love you.

To my nephews, Dylan and Blythe,
and to my niece, Ella
Be nice to your mother. Seriously. You are
going to put her in the loony bin—and then
who will make you sandwiches and kiss your
boo-boos and chauffeur you around town and
buy your birthday presents? And also,
I love you.

ACKNOWLEDGMENTS

To all of you who are not my mother, who are not related to me or owe me money or wouldn't know me if you saw me in the grocery line, and you still bought my books, thank you, thank you, *thank you*. We may never meet, but believe me when I say, I think about you every day. Can I just say it? Yes, it's true. I love you.

You may doubt my love if you have e-mailed me and not gotten a response. I'm usually three months behind in responding to e-mail. And it's not you; it's me. Just ask my friends. I don't e-mail them back, either. It's a character flaw, okay? I'm working on it. Sheesh.

As always, I owe my brilliant editor, Kara, and my brilliant agent, Stephanie, the world covered in chocolate. Thank you for everything.

I'm tremendously grateful to my publicist,

Jessica Growette, who works her fabulous PR mojo on my behalf.

I owe Terri Lugo, Evangeline Anderson, Juanita Kitoaka, Dakota Cassidy, and Renée George so much for their help, their friendship, and their advice. I adore them.

Extra special, chocolate-covered thanks to Cici, Lori, Tricia, Nancy, and Mippy. Mwah.

High fives to Becky Gard and Beth Senters, who have done so much for me, including creating the Consortium's Gift Shop: http://www.cafepress.com /bhconsortium.

My Yahoo! Group rocks. Thanks for hanging out with me every day!

I would also like to thank Keanu Reeves. You are always an inspiration. I have to compete for your affection with my editor, Kara, and my friend Juanita (who saw you in Vancouver from across the street, damn her). I tell them I will share you, but I don't mean it.

Thanks and appreciation to The Atlantic Paranormal Society (TAPS). *Ghost Hunters* has given me and the fam lots of viewing pleasure and plenty of great ideas for stories. My son loves you the best, even though what you do scares the bejeebers outta him.

Everyone should know that Carly Phillips

Acknowledgments

adores me. Yeah, *that* Carly Phillips. I know, I know! It freaked me out, too. She is *so* cool.

Oh, and Gena Showalter totally rules. Hey, Gena! I got a message for you: Drop dead. Hah! See how this works? You write it in one book to *me* and I make sure it gets printed in thousands to *you*. Smooches!

It wouldn't be an acknowledgment without my telling my family: I love, love, LOVE you.

Okay, already. Enough with the mooshy stuff!

Chapter 1

"I ain't a groomin' service," I said, wishing I could still smoke Marlboros. Becoming a vampire cured me of most vices. If I couldn't breathe, I sure as hell couldn't inhale and exhale cigarette smoke. I wanted a donor who smoked, so I'd get a nice fix every time I had a pint. Unfortunately, the Consortium—which was in charge of our little piece of Oklahoma—didn't hire donors who abused their bodies. Yet I hoped for the day I'd find me some nicotine blood.

"You give such good shampoo massages, Patsy," said Darrius, who was a fine-looking male. He could shape-shift into a big, black wolf, too. In either form, Darrius was hard to resist. He'd talked me more than once into a full-body shampoo.

"I own a salon service for people, not mutts."

"If you added animal grooming to your offerings," he said, "you'd make more money."

"You think so?" I liked money almost as much as I liked cigarettes. I couldn't smoke anymore, but I could spend money. I hadn't been jewelry shopping in a dog's age. I looked at Darrius and cackled. *Dog's age.* Wasn't I a hoot?

His green eyes filled with calculation. He sidled closer to me and draped a muscled arm around my shoulders. Oo-wee, I loved it when handsome men flirted with me. Gave me a thrill, it sure enough did. I was forty years old (and would be forever, by God) and not above enjoying the titillation offered by Darrius. Look at him, all cute and wily.

"Oh, all right. But this is the last time." Of course, that's what I said every time Darrius and his ornery brother Drake talked me into a wolfie shampoo. Too cute for their own good, both of 'em. "You know how I feel about watching that shifting bullshit. Go into the back room."

Darrius took two steps before his cell phone

rang. Cursing, he plucked it from the holster on his hip. *"Ja?"*

After listening a moment, he sighed deeply. He shut the phone and reinserted it into the case. "I must take a rain check, *Liebling*. Damian says there is an emergency, but with him, everything is an emergency."

Damian was the third brother; the oldest, by eleven minutes, of triplets. He was head of the Consortium's security, and he protected the borders of Broken Heart fiercely. *He* never asked for a shampoo.

Darrius kissed my cheek, then tapped my nose with his forefinger. "I will be back, Patsy. Then you can rub me all over."

"Promises, promises, stud."

He grinned widely and turned around. I slapped that tight butt so hard my palm stung. He laughed and sauntered out of the salon. Looking at that fine posterior almost made it worth digging out the wolf hair from my tub.

As Darrius exited, cold air gusted through the door and brought with it the promise of snow. Well, what can you do? It was the first week of November, after all. Then again, Oklahoma weather was as fickle as my sister at a half-price shoe sale. Yesterday, the temperature had been a balmy sixty-six degrees.

I turned the sign on the front door to CLOSED. Then I grabbed the broom and started sweeping the clean floor. I'd been feeling off-kilter lately. You know that prickly feeling you get when a storm's coming, but the sky is clear? Whatever it was teased the horizon just enough to keep me clutching my umbrella.

My thoughts drifted to Darrius' suggestion. Grooming services, huh? We had enough lycanthropes around these parts that I could make some extra money as an animal groomer. Business wasn't exactly brisk thanks to the ousting of most of the original residents. Anyone who wasn't a paranormal being or a human donor found themselves elsewhere in a hurry.

I used to have two employees, but they were given new jobs in Tulsa as part of the Broken Heart Citizen Resettlement Program. My nail girl, Linda, got reassigned as an assistant to scientist Dr. Stan Michaels. She was mightily in love with that man, but wouldn't admit it.

Anyway, Broken Heart wasn't exactly a hopping town before the undead took over. Less than a year ago, the only thing that had saved my salon from closing had been the strippers from the Barley and Boob Barn, which had been shut down and razed in June. Aw, hell. I missed those girls. They were fun and raunchy and tipped real good.

I was "life-challenged" because of Lorcan O'Halloran. Diseased by the Taint—a nasty illness that affects only vampires—he'd attempted a radical cure. The cure turned him into a two-legged, hairy, stinky beast. He romped around ol' Broken Heart and killed eleven of us single parents.

Oh, now, don't worry. He's back to being a vampire. He married my friend Eva, Broken Heart's only teacher. She was obviously the forgiving sort, but I still felt uneasy around Lorcan.

The night he attacked me, I'd been outside my shop, smoking a cigarette. If I'd known that was the last smoke I was ever gonna have, I would've enjoyed it a lot more. Anyway, I died. Wham! Knocked down, knocked out, and snacked on. Next night, I woke up on a steel table in a white room, feeling more alive than ever—only to be told I wasn't. And I figured out real quick that I had gained a few new tricks.

It wasn't all bad. My crow's-feet, cellulite, age spots, and the ol' saggies went bye-bye. I had clear, wrinkle-free skin, but no amount of vampifying could rid me of my height, a couple inches shy of six feet, or what my son called "fluffiness." Eva said I reminded her of a Valkyrie, which was some sort of Viking chick who kicked ass. I liked that description, I'll tell you.

The Consortium bought my place and gave it to me lock, stock, and barrel, *and* they paid all bills associated with it and my double-wide, which was twenty feet behind the salon. I didn't have much to do with the money I made, except abuse my credit card on the Home Shopping Network.

"Good evening, Patricia."

The man's voice startled me, but I kept my cool. One thing I'd learned from my ex-husband was that offense was the best defense. "Do you ignore all the signs you read, or just the ones on doors?"

I turned around and leaned on the broom. A man I'd never seen stood inside the doorway, staring at me. And he was *built*, honey. Mm-hmm. I saw the muscles bulging underneath the crisp white shirt opened at the collar. He also wore a pair of tight black jeans and . . . I'll be damned. He had himself a pair of black Prada Croc Sneakers. I liked boots and didn't wear much else. Wilson had shown me a magazine ad with those crocs and said he wanted them. Even though our existence was no longer hand-to-mouth, I couldn't justify buying a pair of shoes that cost twice as much as my mortgage payment.

What was a guy wearing a thousand-dollar pair of kicks doing in my shop? Shoot. What did it matter? Most of the paranormal beings running around our fair town were richer than God.

He didn't seem to mind I was looking him over. As I took his measure, he took mine. His long hair was so white it looked like captured moonbeams. It was drawn into a queue at the back of his neck. If that hair wasn't enough to make the hairstylist in me slobber, then his golden eyes made the woman in me go *mreow*. Those mesmerizing amber orbs reminded me of the sunsets I would never see again.

Damn. He was temptation itself. I was as celibate as a nun because vampires had a hitched-for-a-hundred-years sex clause. My last marriage lasted eighteen years and that was seventeen years, three-hundred-and-sixty-four days longer than it should have. I swore I wouldn't walk down the aisle ever again, much less fall in love. No, thank you.

"Who are you?" I asked.

"My name's Gabriel." He smiled, but it wasn't a nice smile. It was more like an I'll-eat-you-up grin. I shivered all the way to my toes. "Damian sent me. His orders are to secure your beauty shop and to walk you home."

"Why? Are more Wraiths sneaking around or something?"

Wraiths were vampires who thought they should rule the world, being the superior race. Hah. They'd attacked Broken Heart twice and hadn't accomplished much more than pissing off the residents.

He shrugged. "I do what the boss tells me."

I clutched the broom handle, suddenly uneasy. Handsome as he was, I'd never seen him before. Drake and Darrius were always showing up round here for one thing or another, but it didn't make a lick of sense for Damian to send me a guardian.

The man seemed to sense my distress. "You want to call him and ask?" He unclipped his cell phone from his belt and extended it toward me.

I looked at the phone and then at him. If he was willing to let me call Damian and check up on him, then surely he was legit. Yeah, *right*. I may be blond, but I ain't stupid.

"I have him on speed dial." I dug my phone out of my back jeans pocket and flipped it open. The only weapons I had were the broom, my vamp skills, and my charming wit—none of which would disarm him.

I hit the button and put the phone to my ear. Damian picked up on the first ring. *"Ja?"*

"I got a tall drink of water over here who says you sent him."

"You have a what?"

"You are so cliché-challenged," I said. "There's a guy here who wants to hold my hand and walk me home. Did you send him or do I have to whack him with my broom?"

He sighed. "New policy, Patsy. Every Turn-blood has a guardian until . . . well, I say so. Consider him your new shadow. And do not whack him with anything."

Damian hung up. He wasn't much for hellos or good-byes. I put my phone away. "I guess you're my new best pal. Wanna tell me why?"

"You should ask Damian."

"Yeah. It's easier to catch a greased hog than it is to pry information outta that man."

Gabriel's lips turned up into an almost-grin. Mm-mmm. My stomach did a little mambo. Handsome wasn't a good enough word to describe him.

All the same, I felt trapped. I didn't particularly like being bossed around, especially by Consortium puppets. I pretended that him standing there looking all big and powerful and yummy didn't bother me.

"It makes no never mind to me what you do," I lied. "I gotta lock up now."

I finished sweeping up, then turned off the lights. I had to bolt the front door, which meant getting awfully close to Gabriel. Heat emanated off him, as if an invisible fire raged around him. His gaze caught mine; the look in his amber gaze made my stomach jump. Lust zinged through me and he knew it. His lips curved into a feral smile.

I put on my lambskin jacket, then headed out the back door. Gabriel followed and leaned against the wall, watching me lock up. As soon as I was done, I whirled around and hurried across the high grass toward my double-wide. I didn't want the luscious Gabriel within my orbit for too long. I made bad decisions around men like him.

Behind me, I heard a whoosh, and then I heard Gabriel yell. *Whomp. Thud.*

Fear spun through me, but I turned around. And screamed.

The massive creature was at least eight feet tall. He had marbled, gray skin and completely black eyes. His hairless head gleamed in the moonlight. As he took a step toward me, the ground shook. He grinned at me and revealed double rows of needle-sharp teeth.

I didn't see my bodyguard anywhere—until I fell ass over teakettle over him. I landed way too close to the monster's clawed feet.

I scrabbled backward, right into the unconscious form of Gabriel. Some guardian he turned out to be! I scooted over him, knelt by his head, and shook his shoulders. "Hey, you! Get up now!"

The creature watched me in amusement. Dread snaked through me. Gabriel's moonshine hair spilled onto the ground. I detected his shallow breathing and the steady beat of his heart.

"Your boyfriend can take a punch," he said. His voice sounded like thunder. He crossed his huge arms, his expression grim. "Usually that move kills lycans."

Fear chilled me even more than the frigid air. The storm threatening my horizon was here, and damned if I didn't have my umbrella.

"What do you want?" I asked, my voice quivering.

"You."

Horror kept me welded to the ground. I couldn't move. My gaze was glued to the ugly thing bending toward me over Gabriel, who was trapped between us. He enjoyed my terror, the bastard. His curved claws grazed my shoulders as he tried to grab me.

That's when I remembered I was a vampire.

I swung a right hook at his jaw. Pain jolted down my arm on contact, but the strength of the punch made him stagger back. He looked as shocked as I felt.

The growl surprised us both.

My gaze switched to Gabriel. He was awake, his gold eyes filled with fury. He pushed onto his hands and feet. His body arched and his flesh rippled. I heard the snap of bones and the snick of muscles realigning. His clothes and his expensive shoes shredded and fell to the ground.

His face elongated into a large snout filled with sharp teeth. His long hair flowed down his back and joined with the white fur sprouting over every inch of skin.

Snapping and snarling, the white wolf lunged for the monster.

Chapter 2

At this point, I had several options. Scream for help. Pull out my cell phone and call someone. Get up and run for cover.

Unfortunately, I was so discombobulated and scared out of my mind, I didn't make a logical choice. I sat on my butt and watched the fight.

The white wolf was the biggest lycanthrope I'd ever seen, larger and more muscular than even the triplets. He savagely attacked the creature, ripping with his teeth and scratching with his claws.

Black blood seeped from the creature's wounds and smeared the wolf's white fur.

Despite the creature's advantage in both height and strength, his punches and kicks were ineffective. Gabriel's assault was relentless and vicious.

With a roar of frustration, the monster raised his arms to the sky and *poof*. A huge cloud of black smoke erupted from the ground and enveloped him. The noxious smell of sulfur gagged me.

When the air cleared, Evil Dude was gone.

Gabriel sniffed at the blackened soil, digging at burned ground. After a minute, he gave up and turned toward me. God, he was the most beautiful wolfie I'd ever laid eyes on. He limped forward, looking exhausted and torn up. I guess the scary guy had gotten more than a few good licks in.

"Come here," I said.

Panting heavily, his eyes glazed with pain, he plopped down next to me and put his head in my lap. I rubbed his matted fur; then I leaned down and kissed his muzzle. "You did good, hon. Thank you."

Beneath my fingers, his body undulated and I heard the awful snap-snick. Within moments he was human again. And naked. And unconscious.

I needed to get up and out of here. Or call for help or at least get us inside the trailer. Shoot. All the pizzazz had gone out of me. Most vampires got lethargic close to dawn. Sunrise wasn't too far off.

I stood up, grabbed Gabriel under the armpits, and dragged him to the trailer. Even with my vampire strength, he was a handful. Getting him up the three steps and through the door took some doing.

I settled him on the couch.

The headache-inducing music my sixteen-year-old son enjoyed filtered down the hallway. At least he'd kept it down tonight.

My gaze roamed over Gabriel. Oo-wee. He was all kinds of yum. I checked out his package because . . . well, hell, wouldn't you? Now, *that* was a damned fine piece of equipment. I just about drooled over his abdomen and pectorals, all smooth as beige silk. Or would've been if he weren't covered in bruises, cuts, and blood.

"Did you kill him?"

"Oh, God!" I glared at the wizened old woman, who'd been dead herself for almost twenty years. Nonna stood above Gabriel, which she did only because she knew that kind of shit freaked me out.

Yeah. Remember those new tricks I talked about earlier? Well, I can see ghosts. That's my vampire Family's power—seeing earthbound spirits. Yippee.

"Nonna, how many times have I asked you not to pop out of the woodwork like that?"

She shrugged, but her grin was filled with orneriness. That was Nonna, all right. On her eighty-fifth birthday, she'd gone to Vegas and whooped it up. Her favorite thing was playing the one-armed bandits. Old-fashioned to the end, she pulled the handle instead of smacking the big plastic buttons.

Nonna died with one hand curled on the handle and the other hand curled around a Jack and Coke. Nobody noticed she'd passed on for three hours and by then, she was in rigor mortis. They had to remove the handle from the slot machine because they couldn't unclench her wrinkled fingers from the metal bar or from the highball glass. That's how she went to the coroner's office.

Nonna always said she wanted to go in style.

I watched my deceased grandmother poke Gabriel with the toe of her orthopedic shoe, which of course went right through his shoulder. I can't imagine why old people think those white, high-soled shoes look good with workout wear, but there Nonna was, as always, wearing those terrible shoes with her pink velour jogging suit.

"Stop that," I demanded.

"What for?" She did it again, this time sinking her whole shoe into his forehead. She stared at me defiantly. "He cain't feel nothing."

I took out my cell phone and flipped it open. If I was smart, I'd hit the speed dial to Damian. He'd come and take this guy off my hands. Plus, the wolfies needed to know that weird-looking creep was running around town. I shuddered, feeling vulnerable. What if he came back?

Suddenly, I was reluctant to turn over my hero, unconscious or not.

With sunrise imminent, I needed to get to my bedroom. Underneath it was a concrete chamber I access by a trapdoor. I descended a ladder and within five steps, I was at my bed. I was usually tucked in early because I didn't want to risk frying. Undead was better than dead any day of the week.

I leaned over and smacked Gabriel's cheek. He didn't respond at all. Lord, the man was a looker. His lips begged to be kissed. I imagined that mouth of his was real talented. Lust knotted my belly. *Whoa, girl. He's a wolf. You're a vampire. No can do, remember?* Even if I was the dating type, I'd learned in Vampire 101 that dating lycans was one of the big no-no's.

Nonna knelt down, still floating above him;

then she extended her forefingers and jabbed him in the eyes.

"Nonna! Jesus H. Christ!"

"Don't you take the Lord's name in vain," she said sharply, "or you'll go to hell."

"Already there," I muttered.

Nonna popped up outta nowhere this past summer. She said she'd been sent to help me deal with my "gift," and that she'd lived her whole life using her second sight. I had never heard such a load of horseshit, but whatever. She was my grandmother, dead or alive.

"What did you do this time, Patsy?" My other ghostly nemesis arrived on scene. Her name was Dottie. About ten years ago, she'd been murdered by her boyfriend, a trucker named Rocky, who'd strangled her and thrown her off the highway just outside of Broken Heart. He'd never been caught, but that's not why she hung around. She wasn't interested in leaving the earthly plane. She was thrilled to pieces when my psychic energy appeared like a beacon to her lonely soul.

Dottie's red hair was teased ridiculously high. She wore black capris, a V-necked shirt too small to contain her abundant breasts, and high heels. She also carried a huge, black purse. She dug out a pack of Pall Malls and lit up a cigarette. Even though I knew she was doing in death what she'd done in life, it galled me that she could smoke and I couldn't.

"Didn't I tell you not to do that around me?" I asked, irritated.

"Oh, yeah." She blew a ring of smoke into the air. Her gaze wandered over the naked guy. "Who's the hunk?"

"His name is Gabriel. Stop gawking at him."

"Jealous?" Dottie grinned wickedly and continued ogling. Well, what was I gonna do? She was already dead.

"I'm bored. I want to go back to Vegas," Nonna griped. "I almost hit that jackpot."

Dottie cackled. "Yeah, the one in the sky."

"Don't start, you two." I looked down at my naked problem. Just who was guarding who? I figured I should at least get his clothes. Maybe the pants survived his shift.

I headed outside. Nonna came with me, but Dottie stayed in the trailer to drool over my wolf. Man, I was getting tired. I found the place we'd been sitting and looked around. I spotted the black jeans and bent over to scoop 'em up.

My fingers grazed something solid. What the—? I bent over and parted the tall fescue grass, which winter weather had turned brown.

"Who's he?" asked Nonna. She leaned down and squinted at the man. "He's dead."

I could see that for myself. His shirt was in tatters. His mauled chest looked like hamburger meat. Blood spattered his boxer's face, which was square and flat with a nose that had been broken too many times. He looked like a tough bastard.

"Spirit's gone," I said. "You see him, Nonna?"

"Nope."

I looked around, nervous. Had he been attacked by the same creature who'd tried to kill me? I stood up and took out my cell phone. I hit the speed dial to my friend Jessica, who was married to one of the Consortium's founders. Jessica picked up on the third ring. I told her everything that had happened and ended with, "and now I'm standing next to a dead guy."

About two minutes later, Jessica and her husband, Patrick, appeared in a shower of gold sparkles. Dematerialization was a trick most Turn-bloods couldn't do. Frankly, I wasn't interested in dissembling and reassembling my own particles.

Jessica and Patrick looked flushed and rumpled. I figured out that my little phone call had interrupted some bedroom fun. Oops. Envy drove a green streak right through me. I wanted some hot and heavy sex with a stud muffin. My vibrator was gettin' worn out.

Patrick knelt down and examined the man's face.

"I don't recognize him," he said. "But he's definitely a lycan."

About that time, Damian pulled up in his black Ford 350. The rumbling engine died and he jumped out, striding across my weed-filled yard.

He knelt on the other side of the corpse, his expression cold and hard. "Rick." His gaze flicked to mine. "What happened?"

"I don't know. I came out here to get Gabriel's clothes and he was . . ."

Everyone turned and stared at me.

"It's not how it sounds," I said impatiently. "I told you, Jess. My guardian shifted and kicked that monster's ass."

Damian's obsidian eyes flashed with alarm. "What monster?"

"Patsy described the same demon that attacked Simone," said Patrick, frowning.

"Is she okay?" I asked. Simone was Broken Heart's mechanic, and a damned good one. She had some weird water power. I didn't see much use for it, but hell, I had the most useless vampire power of all.

"She'll be fine," said Jessica. "You're lucky Rick fended the demon off."

I was so busy working over the idea of a demon attack, I barely heard her. Then her words penetrated. "Wait. What?" I pointed to Rick. "He's not my guardian."

Damian's eyebrows dipped. "Yes, he is."

"If *he's* my guardian," I said, my voice quivering, "then who the hell is the naked guy in my trailer?"

Chapter 3

Adrenaline spiked in my stomach. Dottie chose that moment to appear, her gaze wandering all over Damian. I looked at Dottie puffing on her nonexistent cigarette and I wanted a smoke so bad, I'd even have settled for a ghost cig.

"Gabriel saved my life." My voice quavered. "If he's not my guardian, why would he do that?"

"Let's go ask him." Damian rose and turned in a fluid movement, which reminded me of his wolf's strength and grace.

He got to the porch before the rest of us. He

unsheathed a gun from his side holster, then opened the door and pointed it inside.

"He's not in there," said Dottie. "Mr. Hunky woke up and went out the window in your bedroom."

Damian apparently figured this out, too. I went inside, followed by Jessica and Patrick.

"Blood," said Damian, looking at my couch. He sniffed the air and frowned. "He's odd, this one. His scent is . . . off."

Gabriel smelled just fine to me, but I didn't have a lycanthrope's nose.

Damian made a call and put the word out about my moon-haired savior. Then we all traipsed outside to stare at the dead guy again.

Patrick and Damian hoisted the big man and carried him to the back of the truck.

Jessica looked at me. I saw the concern in my friend's eyes. "Move into the compound for a while, Patsy. Just until we figure out what's going on."

"I hate the compound." It reminded me of a prison environment. I hadn't seen the inside of a jail cell, mind you, but I'd been on the other side of the window on visiting day.

"We're getting overrun every night with desperate, Tainted vampires. The Ancients are here, which means our security teams are protecting the compound instead of the borders." She rubbed her temples. "To top it off, this week the Wiccans moved into town."

"Witches?"

"Wiccans," she repeated. "We need their protection spells, especially with our security shortage."

I didn't really care who did or didn't live in Broken Heart as long as they left my little piece of sunshine alone. "They got a need for hair care?"

Jessica chuckled. "Probably." Then she looked around. "Are your ghost friends here?"

"Yeah." Ghosts really geeked Jessica out. Right now, Dottie and Nonna were by the truck, watching Patrick and Damian ready Rick's body for transport.

As usual, she carried her fancy half swords tucked into a black hip holster. She clamped the handles as if considering whipping them out. Swords wouldn't do much good against these spirits, but I totally understood the desire to stab anything that annoying.

"I need to get going. I still have to tuck my kids into bed. And make sure Brian brushed his teeth."

I laughed. "A mother's work is never done."

"You said it." She took out her swords and

swung them Xena-style. "I'm taking no chances."

"Hey, Mom. What's up?"

My sixteen-year-old, Wilson, sauntered across the yard, his brown eyes glazed. He stopped about a foot away, but I didn't need my vampire senses to know he'd been smoking dope. My stomach clenched.

"I thought you were inside," I said through gritted teeth. "Where have you been?"

"Out." He infused a lot of hostility into the word.

I glanced at Jessica. I could tell by her expression and crinkled nose that she could smell the marijuana, too. She looked at me, sympathy in her eyes.

"Hi, Wilson," she said. "You doing all right?"

He shrugged and looked away. Jessica didn't seem bothered by his rudeness, but it bothered me. Every time I looked at Wilson, I saw the child and not the struggling teenager. I wanted to hug him into good behavior. But he was past hugs. He was past spankings, too.

I heard the truck start up and looked over my shoulder. Damian backed the truck out of my yard and drove out of sight.

Patrick rejoined us. Dottie and Nonna floated by him; naturally Dottie was checking out his ass. "I'll ask Darrius to watch your place while you rest."

"Thanks."

"Oh!" said Jessica. "We're having our first parent-teacher meeting tomorrow night."

"Yeah. Sure. See you later."

Patrick and Jessica waved good-bye to me. Since they were part of the Family Ruadan, vampires who had fairy blood, they had the ability to fly. I watched my friends rise into the air. Now, that would be a nice power to have. Better than the ability to hang out on a Friday night with ghost hags.

As soon as they were out of sight, I turned a fierce glare on my son. "Don't ever leave the trailer without telling me! God!"

I didn't want to freak him out by saying anything about the demon attack. I only hoped that thing would be caught soon.

The scent of pot rolled over me again and I crinkled my nose. "I told you to stay off that shit, Wilson."

"Don't start, Mom." He walked away, heading toward the trailer.

I marched behind him, feeling helpless and pissed off. "You're going to screw up your brain. You're going to screw up your life."

27

"So what?" Wilson opened the door, hopped the two concrete stairs, and went inside.

I followed. He took off his coat and tossed it onto the couch. He U-turned into the kitchen and opened the fridge. He pulled out a tube of cookie dough, the last of the deviled eggs, and the leftover chicken pot pie. He took his goodies, ignored my smoldering presence, and sat on the couch. He arranged the food on the coffee table, then clicked on the remote.

I stomped to the TV and turned it off. "I'm not through talking to you."

Nonna and Dottie looked at each other, grimaced, and winked out of the trailer. I imagine they didn't want to witness the fight.

"I smoked a joint. Big fuckin' deal."

I bit my tongue. Wilson did more than just smoke some weed now and again. He was prone to drinking himself stupid and he'd tried other drugs. I'd gone through this crap with his daddy. I didn't want to do it with him.

"Doing drugs is a big deal, Wil! Your father—"

"I'm outta here." He scooped up his food and walked down the minuscule hallway to his bedroom. He slammed the door shut. The music shot into migraine-causing decibels.

I wanted to weep, but vampires don't get to

cry. We don't get to eat, either. Or smoke. Or have one stress-relieving vice. Argh!

My undead heart squeezed as I thought about Wilson and the path he'd chosen. I didn't know what to do or how to help him. I was used to being the sober one, the rock in a crisis, the ever-present maid.

But I'd promised myself: never again.

When I was nineteen, I wed pretty boy, empty-headed Sean Donahue. I had been going to beauty school in Tulsa to get my required certifications even though I'd been a part of my grandmother's beauty shop since I could walk.

Sean worked at a gas station near the school. He could charm the fur off a yeti. All it took to get into my pants was a few dozen compliments and a six-pack of Budweiser. Next thing I knew, I was in l-o-v-e.

It took four years to have a child: Wilson. Ten months after he was born, Lynnie came along. She stayed with us for seven weeks, nine days, eight hours, and thirty-seven minutes. Crib death. After that, I had three miscarriages, so I went to the doc's and had my woman parts removed. No more babies. No more losses.

I don't know if losing our daughter and babies exacerbated the wounds Sean already had, but the drinking got worse. I justified his boozing and bad behavior. For a while, I could point to the good intentions he had and the nice things he did.

Yeah, he drinks, but he supports his family.

After ten years, he lost his job at the Tulsa Bus Plant due to absenteeism. Work was cutting into his drinking time. After that, the man couldn't keep a job longer than a month or two.

Yeah, he drinks, but he's a good father.

He stopped playing catch with Wilson, dropped out as Boy Scout leader, forgot birthdays, slept through Christmas mornings, and left me to do the emotional cleanup.

The years passed and the disease of alcoholism did its work; the good man was destroyed inch by inch until only the monster remained. Whatever love and sympathy I had for him was worn away until only grief and anger remained.

One morning, as I cleaned up Sean's vomit for the umpteenth time, I decided fifty more years of this bullshit was more than I could take. The man's first love was booze, and not even losing his home, his wife, and his son was enough motivation for him to stop. We hadn't seen him since the day we signed the divorce papers.

I tried not to think about Sean or about what I had been like with him. We'd been better off without him, but finally giving up and filing for divorce felt like peeling off my own skin with a cheese grater.

I couldn't rely on Wilson to stay in his room while I slept, but he couldn't leave the town without running into one of the wolves. Yet, even without access to the outside world, he was still finding a way to get drugs. I wasn't too keen on asking the Consortium any favors, but they were efficient problem solvers. I'd been thinking lately I would swallow my pride and ask for their help.

I tugged on my oversized football jersey and crawled into bed. There was something to be said about vampire sleep. Worry and guilt couldn't keep me tossing and turning.

The undead sleep like . . . well, the dead. When the sun rises, we have no choice but to shut our peepers and lie down. And when the sun sets, we wake up ready for a blood breakfast.

Ever since I got undead, I haven't dreamed.

Until tonight.

In my dream, I sat at a small table that was one of many in an outdoor café. Daylight slanted across the marble surface and I touched it with one finger. I inhaled the scent of strong coffee and cinnamon rolls.

Across from me sat a young woman wearing a halter top and jeans. She had the bluest eyes I'd ever seen. Her skin was creamy, her lips rose red. Her dark hair hung in careless ringlets. She took my hand and turned it over, tracing the lines.

"You must follow your heart, Patsy. Don't let past disappointments shape your future," she said with an Italian accent. "You have a great destiny, one that you share with Gabriel."

"I don't understand."

"You will." She winked at me.

The dream shifted. . . .

I stood at a picture window in a room I didn't recognize. I looked over my shoulder and saw a huge, four-poster bed. The covers were messed up, as if whoever slept there had just gotten up. A fire crackled in the big, stone hearth, where two red wing chairs faced its warmth. I returned my gaze to the window.

Outside, the full moon danced along the tree-tops. I was dressed in a luxurious silk robe. I could feel my lungs fill with air and my heart beat steadily in my chest.

My belly felt heavy. I looked down and gasped. I was pregnant. Impossible. I pressed my hands against my roundness and felt a tiny foot kick against my palm.

I wanted to weep.

To my surprise, I did. I closed my eyes and let the tears course down my cheeks.

Fingertips brushed away the wetness. I opened my eyes and met Gabriel's sun-fire gaze.

Lord-a-mercy. He stared at me with such longing, such love, I wanted to give him anything he asked.

"What's wrong, sweetheart?"

"Nothing," I whispered. Happiness welled within me. "Everything is perfect."

His ravenous grin reminded me that he was a werewolf. I felt like he might devour me in that moment. As if to confirm my fears (or hopes?), he pressed his hot mouth to mine.

And then the dream melted away and I fell into the soft darkness of vampire sleep.

The Story of Ruadan the First

As Written by Lorean O'Halloran

Once there was a great warrior-magician whose name was Ruadan. He was the son of magician-healer Brigid and warrior-prince Bres.

Brigid was born the daughter of Dagda, all-father to the Tuatha de Danann, and of Morrigu, the crow queen. Bres was born the son of Fomhoire prince Elatha and of Tuatha de Danann princess Eriu. So, the families bound together their children so that they might rule as one.

Many believed Bres would bring peace to the troubled nations. When he came of age, he married Brigid to solidify his bond with the Tuatha de Danann. In time, he was made King of Eire.

But Bres was a foolish ruler, ignorant of his people's suffering and unjust in his judgments. The sons of Tuatha de Danann rose up against him and took his crown, banishing him. In defeat, Bres returned to his father's kingdom.

Bres was too prideful to turn away from the dishonor shown to him by the Tuatha de Danann, no matter how deserved. He vowed to take back what had been taken from him and to once again rule Eire.

Brigid wanted peace between the Fomhoire and the Tuatha de Danann. Without her husband's knowledge, she sought her mother's counsel. Morrigu foresaw the future and told her daughter the truth: The Tuatha de Danann would triumph over the Fomhoire, but not before Brigid lost her husband and their sons, Ruadan, Iuchar, and Uar.

The Tuatha de Danann had a magical well that instantly healed their warriors so long as they had not suffered a mortal blow. Created by a goldsmith named Goibniu, the well was safeguarded by spells and men alike. "Kill the builder of the well," said Bres to his sons, "and destroy its magic . . . and the Tuatha de Danann will fall."

So it came to pass that Ruadan's wife, Aine, bore twin boys, Padriag and Lorcan. Satisfied that his family was safe, Ruadan and his brothers sailed to the Isle of Eire to fulfill his father's plan.

The brothers used stealth and cunning to break through the defenses of their enemy. While Iuchar and Uar battled those who guarded the well, Ruadan stabbed Goibniu with the fae swords. But Goibniu, though mortally wounded, thrust his spear into Ruadan's chest and felled the warrior.

Near death, Ruadan arrived in his homeland and was taken to his mother. She used all her magic and healing arts, but could not save her son. The very same night Ruadan breathed his last, Brigid received word of the deaths of Iuchar and Uar. She fell to her knees and wailed with such sorrow that anyone who heard the sounds knew a mother's heart had been rent from her.

Morrigu heard the keening of her daughter, so she turned into a crow and flew to the land of the Fomhoire. Though the dark queen craved chaos over tranquility and war over peace, she felt pity for her daughter and offered one chance for Brigid to regain her son.

"Give Ruadan a cup of my blood, but be

warned! When he awakes, he will not live as a man, but as a *deamhan fola*. He will never again walk in the light. He will not consume food or drink, but shall siphon the blood of the living. Neither will he have breath nor beat of heart. Never will he sire another child by his own seed."

"Is there no good to be wrought then, Mother?"

"Where there is dark, there is also light. Ruadan will never age. He will heal from even the most grievous of wounds. He will know the thoughts of those he loves. And he will be a warrior none can defeat. He is of the Fomhoire and of the Tuatha de Danann, and those skills and magic will always be his to wield."

So blinded by grief was Brigid, so badly did she want her son to live again, that she agreed to her mother's terms. But still, Morrigu was not satisfied.

"Should Ruadan drain a man and replenish him with Tainted blood, he shall Turn. Your son will create others and he will rule a master race long after all whom you know and love turn to dust and ash. Even knowing this, will you still give him my blood to drink?"

And again, Brigid agreed without hesitation. Morrigu cut her wrist and bled into a silver goblet. Brigid lifted her son's head, opened his mouth, and poured every drop of her mother's blood into him.

When Ruadan awoke, he was *deamhan fola*.

Bres, devastated by the loss of his sons, went himself to the Isle of Eire to wreak vengeance on his enemy, but he, too, was killed. Finally, the Tuatha de Danann triumphed over the Fomhoire, and there came to pass an uneasy peace between their peoples.

But Aine was frightened of the creature her husband had become and refuted him, calling him demon and eater of flesh. He wished only happiness for his family and so, he bartered with Aine. If she returned with his mother to the Isle of Eire and raised their sons as Tuatha de Danann, he would leave them alone.

For twenty-five years, Ruadan wandered the world. He made six others of his kind. And then, because he longed to see his sons, Ruadan broke his promise. He visited his twin boys—and both were killed. He turned them into *deamhan fola*, and together, they left the Isle of Eire.

Ruadan summoned his first six *deamhan fola* to a meeting, and they created the Council. They labored to create laws for their people and bound all *deamhan fola* with magic and by oath to uphold these laws. Those who broke faith with their Families faced banishment . . . or death.

And so it was that Brigid's son fulfilled her mother's prophecy.

He was the creator of the *deamhan fola*.

He was ruler over all.

He was Ruadan the First.

Chapter 4

I made breakfast every evening around seven p.m. Wilson almost always hung around long enough to scarf food down. Then we would get into the usual where-are-you-going argument and he'd stomp out of the trailer, and I'd go to work.

We sat at the foldout table in the kitchen. Wil shoveled eggs into his mouth while I mentally lamented my inability to suck down a pot of coffee like I used to when I was human.

"Who's Gabriel?" he asked.

Startled, I looked at him and felt myself blush—which wasn't easy for a vampire to do. "I don't know what you're talking about."

He smirked at me. "I heard you last night, all the way from the kitchen. 'Oh, Gabriel,' " he said in a high-pitched, girly voice. " 'Oh! *Oh!*' "

"Stop it!"

"I know about sex, Mom." He shoved a deviled egg into his mouth and glared at me while he chewed it. "When are you going to introduce me to your boyfriend?"

"He's not my boyfriend. He's just—" *A hot shape-shifting, bad-ass, yummilicious man.* I'd be damned if I admitted that I'd dreamed about a man I'd met for all of two seconds.

"Jessica wants me to go to the parent-teacher meeting tonight," I said, switching to a subject neither one of us much liked. "Why don't you go with me? Maybe you can talk to Eva about getting caught up on your studies—"

"Not this again!" He slammed his fork against the table. Egg bits went flying. "I don't want to go to school, okay? It's lame and I'm no good at it."

"You're smart. You could do well if you wanted."

"Yeah, if I *wanted*." He scooted out from the table. "I'm old enough to make my own decisions. Why don't you just leave me the hell alone?"

He stomped into the living room and threw

on his coat. Without another word to me, he left the trailer, slamming the door behind him. Despair clawed at me and I put my head in my hands.

Breakfast. Fight. Cleanup. The Donahue clan's morning events were right on schedule.

The phone rang.

I relished the idea of a telemarketer. I could rip the poor bastard a new asshole and not feel a whit of guilt about it. I left the kitchen and picked up the mobile sitting on the coffee table.

I plopped onto the couch. "Hello?"

"Hi, Patsy," said my only and much younger sister, Millie. "Guess what?"

She didn't wait for me to guess. Instead, she shrieked, "I'm getting married!"

"What the fuck for?" I blurted.

Her pause was too damned long and I knew I had gut-punched her. Our parents had died when Millie was sixteen and I was thirty-four. We were eighteen years apart, which meant my mother raised two only children. Millie lived with me until she turned legal. Her college fund kicked in and off she went to Texas for an education.

We had a hate/hate relationship. As her older sister, I was already bossy. When I took over parenting duties, she resented the hell out of me. In

May, I went to her college graduation, wished her luck, and other than a birthday card when I hit four-oh in June, I hadn't heard from the ungrateful whelp.

"I'm in love," she said finally, her excitement gone. "Not *every* marriage is crummy."

"Keep telling yourself that."

She sucked in a breath, then said, "Hang on a minute. I have another call."

I heard the click of call waiting. Damn. Now I had time to think about how mean I was acting. Millie gettin' married. Gawd.

I heard another click. Then Millie said, "I knew you were going to act like this! Damn it, Patsy! You're my only family. I want you to be happy for me."

I wanted to be happy for her, too. But I just couldn't work up the appropriate emotion. "What's his name?"

"Ronald Meyers. He's a doctor." Her voice went dreamy all over again. "We met in the emergency room."

"What? Why? What happened?" My sisterly-motherly impulses kicked into overdrive.

"This is why I don't like telling you anything. You always overreact. I've been dating him for a year, but I didn't tell you because . . . well, *because*."

No wonder she hurried me off after the graduation ceremony in May. She didn't want me to meet Mr. Right and give him the once-over. I had a habit of scaring off her boyfriends.

"So when's the Big Day?" I asked.

"The first week of December."

"Next year?"

"No. This December."

My sister was all about the dream wedding. Unless she'd been planning it for the whole time she'd been dating this Robert Meyers, then something was up.

"Either he's terminally ill or you're..." I nearly swallowed my tongue. Oh, dear Lord. *"Millie, are you pregnant?"*

"I think they can hear you in Canada." Millie let out a huge sigh. "Yes, damn it! I'm pregnant."

I couldn't form any words. My little sister was getting married. She was preggers. Well, maybe my weird dream had been a portent of my sister's news. Given my lack of womb, not to mention my undeadness, I'd never have another kid.

I leaned my head against the back of the couch and closed my eyes. I needed a cigarette. A whole pack. No, no. A *carton* of Marlboros.

"I knew you were going to do this," said Millie. "I told Robbie that you would be pissed off. And he wanted to have the ceremony in Broken Heart!"

Jesus God! This situation kept getting worse and worse. "You can't get married here."

How the hell would I explain the vampires, the wolfies, and the Consortium? The blood-sucker mafia wouldn't let my sister, her fiancé, and mortals from Dallas into the town for a wedding. It didn't matter that Millie was born and raised here. Broken Heart no longer belonged to the humans.

Millie burst into tears. "You can't tell me where to have my wedding! It's the closest I'll get to having Mom and Dad there."

"So, you're getting hitched in the graveyard?"

"You're heartless," she screeched. Then she slammed the phone down.

I listened to the dial tone for a long moment before opening my eyes. I turned off the phone receiver and tossed it onto the coffee table.

"Y'know, you never could cook worth a damn." Nonna floated near my left shoulder and watched me do the breakfast dishes.

I didn't respond to her comment because Nonna believed that a good cook made every-thing from scratch and I believed in using tech-nological advances to make my life easier.

"Lay off, you old bat," said Dottie in a lazy voice. She sat on the kitchen table cross-legged and stared out the tiny window. "Who cares about runny eggs? She's got man problems."

Jerks. Despite their opinions about my kitchen skills, I knew how to put meals together. I turned around and pointed the soapy spatula at Dottie. "What do you mean 'man problems'? Are you talking about Wilson?"

"Naw. I was talking about your mystery man." She pulled out her Pall Malls and set about lighting up a cig. She puffed away, unconcerned about tormenting me.

"And?" I nearly ground my teeth into pulp waiting for her to respond.

Dottie shrugged, which jiggled her considerable cleavage. If I could get ghosts to do my bidding, I would've sent her to track down Gabriel. Nonna might've done it, but she gets distracted too easily.

I tried to shake off the dread snaking through me. Why had Gabriel pretended to be my guardian? Another terrifying thought occurred: What if he had killed Rick? I hoped it wasn't true. But why would he kill another lycan? And why would he lie about who he was? Did the demon show up before Gabriel could . . . well, do whatever he'd planned?

Dottie blew a stream of smoke into the air. "Are you going to find ol' Gabe?"

"Why should I? Gabriel isn't my problem."

Her left eyebrow quirked. "If you say so."

Putting thoughts of Gabriel and his whereabouts out of my mind, I took a shower and got dressed.

Even though I was stuck with the same haircut for all eternity, my blond locks still took some wrangling. Today, I put it in a French braid.

I dressed in a T-shirt that proclaimed my love for the Dixie Chicks, my faded jeans, and my snakeskin boots.

I wondered where Wilson had gone and when he'd get back. He was darn near grown and I felt as though I'd failed him. An alcoholic father who'd abandoned him and a mother who was the walking dead . . . jeez! Was it any wonder Wilson had a few issues? God, I missed him. I missed the way we used to be together.

When he was younger, he told me stories about ninjas hiding in the forest and secret spies who met in the school basement. He was quick-witted and smart, but I supposed living in a home where your parents fought all the time and your dad drank himself into a coma while watching CNN could suck the joy right out of your world.

When Wilson went to junior high, he just . . . fell apart. He stopped studying, he got into trouble in his classes, and after a while, he started skipping school. Forget talking to me. No punishment worked. No reward. No nothing. How do you make someone care again? How do you break through someone else's walls, built by pain and loss?

We often stood in the same room, not talking to each other, and I would always feel like someone had punched me in the gut.

I lost my son.

And I didn't know how to get him back.

It wasn't fair, you know, to blame Sean for everything that went wrong. He didn't decide to be an alcoholic. But he'd sure decided he didn't want to be sober.

I was so lonely. Getting free of my marriage to Sean was like breaking the surface of the water after nearly drowning. I enjoyed that freedom. Still did. Sometimes, I found myself thinking about finding someone who could really share my life, all its sorrows, disappointments, joys, and thrills.

That was heady stuff, right there. Dangerous, too, especially when Gabriel came dancing into my thoughts. Not that I believed someone as heartbreakingly handsome as Gabriel could really be mine. Shoot. I would have bet my subscription to *Cosmo* that I was *not* Mr. Yummy's dream gal.

Oh, I didn't suffer from self-esteem issues, but I also knew my rank in the world. I lived in a trailer, I loved country music, I was a beautician, and to tie it all together, I was blond. Plus, I lived in a small town, I had no college education, and I could give a damn about politics, religion, or causes.

I wandered around the trailer, thinking I should open up the shop. Not that I had any appointments. I'd already done inventory umpteen times and I'd cleaned until there wasn't anything left to clean. I felt restless and bored. Being a beautician and running the family business had been my only dream for so long, I just couldn't fathom not doing it. I'd already given up on my marriage. I didn't want to give up my career, too. How many pieces of a person could be stripped away before there was nothing left?

I passed by the wall clock in the living room and groaned. Oh, man. Jessica expected me to attend the first meeting of the Paranormal Parent Teacher Association in an hour. There wasn't really a point to my attending the shindig. Even though the new night school opened in October, Wilson had never attended. Besides, the school was in the compound and we've established how much I hate that place.

Okay, forget the PPTA meeting. Plus, I was starving. I decided to put up the CLOSED sign in the shop, and then head over to my donor's house.

I put on my coat and stepped onto my tiny front porch.

"Patsy." The voice was not one I had heard before.

The tall, handsome man was caramel-skinned and shaved bald. His eyes were brown and he seemed, I dunno, wise. He was dressed in a very nice black suit and sported an electric blue tie.

"Who are you?" I asked.

"I am Khenti. Your Master."

Chapter 5

"My *Master?*"

Khenti must've seen my I-don't-fucking-think-so expression, because he laughed. "I am the one who Turned you."

"Oh."

He seemed to be waiting for more.

"Er . . . thank you?"

He laughed again. "You're welcome. We don't have much time and I have much to teach you."

"You mean now?"

"Yes. Koschei won't wait much longer to attack in earnest. You're not the only Turn-blood who's been targeted." He rubbed his hands together. "So, first things first."

"Well, all right." I stepped off the porch and joined him in the calf-high grass.

"Before my father went to ground, he said that I should not make too many vampires. Our abilities make us more dangerous. In other Families, they have nearly a thousand children. The Family Amahté has fewer than a hundred. Except for you and me, there is not another Amahté vampire on this continent."

My mouth dropped open. "There's not another vampire like us in America?"

"Most of the Family Amahté resides in Africa, Turkey, and a few in Greece. As you know, Turning is not easy. Most humans do not survive the process, so that is another reason we remain small in numbers."

I hadn't known that. I hadn't exactly made an effort to learn the history of my sect, much less what I could do with my abilities. I felt so ashamed. I had been so determined to hold on to my old life that it never occurred to me I was needed in this new one.

"Why are we so dangerous?" I asked. "Sitting around talking to ghosts isn't exactly the same as throwing fireballs or controlling people's minds."

"You can command the spirits who remain on the earthly plane, not just chat with them. You can also raise the dead, Patsy."

"I can bring people back?"

"Ah. Well, you can reinsert souls into bodies, but I don't recommend it. You can reanimate bodies without souls. They're like puppets. They'll do exactly as you ask, no less and no more."

I couldn't fathom why anyone would want to make a bunch of decomposing corpses walk around. Sure, there was a high yuck factor. And as the first line of defense in a war . . . oh, I got it now. I remember Eva telling me once how during castle sieges in medieval times people would throw the dead over the walls. How would you like a body, all disgusting and bug-filled, falling on you?

"So, I could raise a zombie army, if I wanted."

Khenti laughed. "Yes, if you wanted."

Of all the people in Broken Heart Khenti could've given his gift, he chose the tall blonde who was hell with scissors and not much else.

"Why me?" I asked, my voice catching. I didn't feel worthy, not one bit. "I'm nobody."

"I'm nobody! Who are you?
Are you nobody, too?

55

Then there's a pair of us—don't tell!
They'd banish us—you know!
How dreary to be somebody!
How public like a frog
To tell one's name the livelong day
To an admiring bog!"

I looked at Khenti, who seemed so pleased with his recitation. He smiled. "You see, Patsy? You are not a nobody, unless you believe you are."

Well, hell. Why didn't he just say that instead of spouting off those rhymes?

"I love Emily Dickinson, don't you?"

"Er . . . is she a vampire?"

"She was a poet," said Khenti. "And no, she was not a vampire. She penned those words, Patsy." He sighed. "Perhaps you should pick up a book more often."

He was probably right. Though I doubted it would be a poetry book.

"I have a question. If we get our powers from the seven Ancients, then why aren't we all just from Ruadan's line?"

"He went to Morrigu and asked for the secret for making others of his kind. She told him how to do it. Then she gave him a gift. With a spell she taught him, he could choose six others to

Turn who would be his equals with their own powers. I'm sure she hoped it would cause strife and grief among our kind."

"Um . . . who's Morrigu? And why would she want to cause strife?"

Khenti looked amazed. "You don't know the history of Ruadan the First?"

"No." I sighed. "Yeah, yeah I *know*. I need to read more books."

"Indeed. Morrigu is Ruadan's grandmother, an ancient goddess who gave him her dark blood and made him the first vampire. She's the goddess of chaos." He smiled at me. "I'll teach you what you must know to use your powers effectively. Are you ready?"

"Okay," I said, determined to master my skills and make him proud. I couldn't whine about my old life anymore. It was gone. And it was time that I embrace what I had become . . . and what was in store for me as a vampire of the Family Amahté.

Khenti made me memorize words and gestures associated with my powers. By the time we'd finished, I could call a ghost and direct him to do my bidding. I could help those who were lost find the Light. I could make a dead body rise from its grave and do the boot-scoot boogie if I wanted.

"Patsy, you are an able student and a good woman."

Pleased with his compliment, I grinned. "Thanks. You're not so bad yourself."

He took my hands into his. "There is one other Amahté vampire in America. In Las Vegas. Do you know the casino-resort called the Pharaoh's Tomb?"

"Yes," I said, shaking my head in wonderment. "That's the place where my nonna breathed her last. At the slot machines."

"I'm aware," said Khenti. "It is how I knew to call her to you. You see, I own the Pharaoh's Tomb. There is a gateway of sorts there. And I am especially connected to those who pass away near its borders."

"You got my nonna to leave the Great Beyond?"

"Yes, though I did think she would be more help. She is distracted rather easily."

"You ain't kidding," I laughed.

"I opened a museum last year. One of its most popular displays is a gold sarcophagus that belongs to Pharaoh Amenemhet II."

"But it's your father in there," I guessed.

"Yes. I've kept his location secret from everyone, to protect his resting place. However, with Koschei just getting warmed up . . . it is probably best if someone else knows the secret. In case something happens to me."

"Hey, you've lasted four thousand years," I said.

"Nothing lasts forever, Patsy. Not even vampires." He smiled sadly. Then he hugged me.

I felt the familiar tingle of magic. Oh, crap.

Within moments, we appeared at the edge of a field. I looked around and shuddered. Why had he brought me here, of all places?

"Next time, warn me, will you?" I pulled out of his arms and shivered. "I really don't enjoy having my atoms scattered all over the place."

Khenti chuckled. "It's time to practice what I taught you."

"I've never tried to use my power on purpose. The ghosts usually find me. And some of 'em don't go away." I glared at Dottie and Nonna who popped next to me.

Khenti bowed to them. "Ladies." Then he turned to me. "It will be a good exercise for you. If Johnny and Nefertiti are trapped here, reliving their last moments, use your powers to free them."

He was making me nervous. He kept looking around and frowning. I especially didn't like it when he stared up at the sky, his expression worried.

Dottie and Nonna floated next to me. Both of them were fascinated with Khenti.

"You're cute," said Dottie for the millionth time. "You say you're not married?"

Khenti's teeth flashed white as he smiled. "No."

"Oh, stop it," I said. "He doesn't date ghosts, for God's sakes!"

"His loss," she said, and she winked at him.

Reluctance mired me to the ground. I didn't really want to go over there and tap Johnny on the shoulder, so to speak.

Johnny Angelo, 1950s movie star and reluctant vampire, believed for the last fifty years that he had turned a cat into a vamp. What he hadn't known until a couple months ago was that the feline was really Nefertiti, the woman who had seduced and bound him. Basically, she used him as a shield to protect her own sorry, evil hide. Y'see, she had been Koschei's number one henchman. Henchwoman. Whatever.

Johnny hadn't chosen to be Turned or to be married to a vampire. I felt sorry for him.

As we approached the spot, I felt my stomach take a dive. The first time I watched Johnny and Nefertiti relive the murder-suicide, I nearly threw up.

I didn't know if I could pry them from each

other long enough to ask either one any questions, much less figure out how to get them into the Light.

We all watched the ugliness unfold.

"All these years . . . and there she is," Johnny whispered. His hair was matted, his clothes dirty, and his smile grim. He'd been searching for his wife nonstop for weeks. "Nefertiti."

Nefertiti stared at Johnny. "Oh, my husband," she cried. "I wanted only to protect you."

"Liar," said Johnny softly. He strode forward and grabbed a fistful of Nefertiti's silky locks. "You cursed me. I watched my pregnant fiancée marry someone else. Another man raised our daughter." He twisted the knot of hair tighter, but she didn't flinch. "I hate you."

"I gave you immortality." She smirked at him. "You will live forever because of me."

"You're wrong. I'm just a walking dead man." Johnny's other hand rose and in a flash of silver, Nefertiti's head separated from her shoulders.

Johnny tossed Nefertiti's head onto the ground. His lips curved into the famous half smile that had made him such a movie-star heartthrob half a century ago. "I'm free."

Nefertiti's corpse exploded into dust.

And then, Johnny crumbled into ash.

I pressed my hand against my squirming stomach. Johnny wasn't free. He hadn't passed on to the next world. He was trapped in the cycle of his own death. For those who thought vampires were soulless, I dared them to look at this tragedy and still believe it.

"Any clue what I'm supposed to do?" I asked.

"You're the ghost whisperer," said Dottie. Then she cackled. "Why don'cha call Jennifer Love Hewitt? Maybe she can help."

I looked at Dottie and figured if I was going to experiment, I'd start with her. "Go away," I demanded in my vampire glamour voice, which I hadn't much call to use.

She dropped her ghost cig, she was so surprised. Not at my words, because I'd said them often enough. No, she started twisting and squeezing. She looked as if she were getting sucked through a straw.

Then she was gone.

Nonna glared at me. "Don't you even think about doing that to me, young lady."

"Or what?" I sassed. Then I waved my hand to ward off the lecture. "I ain't gonna send you away."

I'd probably ask Dottie to come back. I was getting used to them. I kinda liked having them around. Mostly.

"Focus, Patsy." I could tell Khenti was feeling a tad impatient with me.

I walked to the spot where the tragedy was playing out again.

"Liar," said Johnny softly. He strode forward and grabbed a fistful of Nefertiti's silky locks.

"Um . . . hi, Johnny!" I waved at him, afraid he would take that hidden sword and decapitate Nefertiti before we could chat. "Yoo-hoo!"

He looked up, blinking as if he'd been asleep. The rest of the scene around him was frozen. Nefertiti stared up at him, that awful smirk on her pretty mouth.

"What's going on?" he asked in a hoarse voice. "Where am I?"

Chapter 6

"**Y**ou're in Broken Heart at the place where you murdered Nefertiti—and yourself." I gave Johnny the news as gently as possible.

He looked down into the beautiful face of the vampire who'd Turned him. "I killed her. And I'm not free." He looked at me, his gaze filled with pain. "Why?"

"Why isn't he free of Nefertiti?" I asked Khenti. I didn't want to break eye contact with Johnny. I wasn't sure how long he'd give me his attention and wanted no excuse for him to go back to what he'd been doing.

"The magic of the binding is one of the

strongest spells ever constructed. The hundred years must be fulfilled, whether on this plane or the next."

"Fifty years more," he cried. "With *her*."

"Wait!" I screamed as he lifted the blade. "God knows she deserves it, honey. I'm here to help."

"You want to help? Sever my ties with this bitch."

"I'm sorry," I said. "I can't."

Johnny let his sword fly. Nefertiti's head came free of her body. One after the other, they exploded into ash.

I couldn't bear to see it all play out again. I turned and ran.

I stopped in a copse of trees and leaned against one, trying to get my thoughts settled. My stomach was gurgling something fierce, a mix of hunger and nausea.

Khenti laid a hand on my shoulder. "Patsy. Are you all right?"

"I'm wonderful." I straightened and turned. "They're caught in a horrifying situation—all because of the damned binding spell created by the Ancients."

"We did what we thought was best for our people," said Khenti. "Why did you talk only to Johnny?"

I had instinctively woken Johnny from that awful business. I understood why now. "He's the only one who can control her. If I ask her anything directly, she breaks out of the death cycle. She may know a trick or two about freeing herself from that drama. You really want the ghost of that evil bitch roaming around Broken Heart? Who knows what she could do."

The thought of what Nefertiti might be capable of as a free spirit chilled me to the marrow. She could possess others or even contact Koschei. I shuddered and wrapped my arms around myself.

"Very good," said Khenti. He nodded approvingly.

I was glad he wasn't too pissed. I felt like I'd failed miserably. "I didn't exactly succeed," I pointed out. "They're still trapped."

"It's worth trying again," he said. "But not tonight."

"Yes," said a thundering voice behind me. "You have a much bigger problem."

Khenti and I turned. The gray-skinned demon who'd attacked me last night leaned against an oak tree, grinning. "Remember me, Patsy?"

Nonna screeched like a banshee and shot up

into the branches of the oak. I backed away, scared witless. This was the same demon who'd tried to get at me before. His black gaze followed me as he licked his leathery lips. Jesus. What was he gonna do? Put me on the dinner menu?

"Andhaka," said Khenti. "So, your mistress has aligned with Koschei."

The demon shrugged. "What are you going to do? Throw ghosts at me?" He laughed. "You have no power over me."

"Well, then," said Khenti, discarding his jacket, "I'll just have to kill you."

The demon launched from the tree with a roar and headed straight for Khenti. I skittered backward and yelped.

"Get out of here, Patsy," cried Khenti. He ducked another punch, then landed a nice one in the demon's abdomen.

"Behind you," screamed Nonna from the tree. Then she popped out of sight. I guess watching people wallop each other was too much for her.

Her warning came a split second too late. A hand gripped my shoulder and I screeched as I tried to wrest free.

Desperate, I grabbed the wrist holding me. The moment my hand made contact, it felt like fire shot through me. The heat raced through my every nerve ending. I felt electrified. The power surge hurt something fierce, but it also gave me strength.

I pulled free from the iron grip and whirled around to see a thin, short woman. *She* was the one causing me so much trouble? She looked like a spring breeze would knock her over. Her cinnamon skin was smooth and ageless, and her brown eyes shone as cold and flat as river stones. Her black robes fluttered around her. Her gray hair, which she wore in a single braid, shone like silver in the moonlight.

"We choose our fates," she said in a lyrical voice. "Prophecy is nothing more than men making their own hopes a reality."

"Uh . . . ooookay." I backed away. To our left, the demon and Khenti battled. I smelled the rusty scent of blood, heard the groans and oomphs as blows were delivered as well as the scrabbling of feet against the leaf-strewn ground.

"I don't want to hurt you," I said.

"You cannot. I am Durga the Ancient and I rule demonkind."

Oh, shit.

I heard Khenti scream. I turned away from Durga, which was stupid, but I couldn't help it.

I saw that the demon had pinned Khenti to the ground. His huge, gray hand gripped the Egyptian's neck.

"Finish it!" commanded Durga.

"Durga," gasped Khenti. "Do not do this! You know that Koschei is *droch fola*. He has no soul."

Durga was unmoved by this logic. Koschei may not have had his soul, but this lady didn't have a heart. "Finish him, minion."

Andhaka squeezed Khenti's neck harder and I realized that he meant to do so until my friend's head came off. Nausea gurgled in my stomach.

Durga hit me across the face. I sailed through the air and landed with a *whomp* on the hard ground.

My whole body felt as though I'd gone through a shredder, but I managed to sit up. Blood dripped down my temple and my vision blurred for an instant.

Across the field, I saw the white wolf streaking toward us. Durga saw the direction of my gaze, and turned.

I cheered when Gabriel knocked her flat on her back and clamped her throat.

Durga knew when she'd been beaten. She did the disappearing-vampire trick. One second she was there and the next Gabriel was sitting among the fading gold sparkles.

He turned his attention to the demon, advancing slowly, snarling and growling.

"You again!" shouted the demon. "Mongrel!"

Gabriel leapt for Andhaka and sank his teeth into the demon's shoulder. Andhaka was forced to let go of Khenti's neck so that he could swipe at the attacking wolf.

His claws made vicious contact. Gabriel yipped in pain and darted back, which gave Khenti an opportunity to strike. He smacked the demon in the chest with both hands, and Andhaka flew backward.

Gabriel launched himself at the discombobulated creature. Black smoke roiled from the ground. Andhaka howled in rage, and then *poof* . . . he was gone.

Khenti sat up, staring down at his ruined suit. Gabriel padded to me and sat down. He licked my face and yipped.

"Thank you," I said. I grabbed his ruff and planted a kiss on his furry nose. "You have impeccable timing."

He barked his agreement.

Gabriel's eyes held mine. He licked my face again, and then he was off, running for the cover of trees on the other side of the clearing.

"I owe the white wolf my life," said Khenti as he got to his feet.

"Yeah. Me, too." Again. I stood up and dusted off my clothes.

"We should go to the compound," said Khenti. "It's safest there."

"Hell, no. I hate that place. I'm going home, demon or no demon."

"Then at least let me take you there and see to your safety."

"You mean the sparkle thing?"

He nodded and held out his arms.

Well, crap.

I was starving, but I'd promised Khenti to stay put until my new guardian arrived. I opened the back door to the shop and locked it behind me, then flipped on the lights.

Nonna was still upset about my telling that cigarette-smoking tart to vamoose, so I said, "Dottie, come back!"

She shimmered into one of the styling chairs and gave me the evil eye. "Never do that again. It was terrible! Just this big white space with uncomfortable chairs and old magazines. It was like being in a waiting room where your name is never called."

"Really? Then I suggest you think twice about pissing me off."

She stuck out her tongue at me, Nonna laughed, and we were all friends again.

I was halfway across the shop when someone pounded on the back door. I nearly jumped out of my skin. My first thought was that the demon had returned, but I realized he wouldn't knock. I returned to the back door and yelled, "Who is it?"

"Gabriel. Please, let me in!"

Oh my God! My fingers clenched the bolt, but I didn't turn it.

"You're not my guardian," I shouted. "You lied to me."

"I only wanted to protect you. I swear it."

"Why?"

"Do we have to talk through this blasted door? Please, Patsy. Trust me."

He'd come to my rescue twice. I'd sure love to know why. Before I could talk myself out of it, I unbolted the door and swung it open. Gabriel nearly fell into my arms, but managed to stagger inside on his own. He looked a mess. He wore only a pair of jeans. His magnificent chest had been clawed. Blood dripped onto the floor.

I slammed the door shut and locked it again.

Gabriel sank to his knees, swaying. His face was tight with pain.

I knelt down. My hands hovered over his shoulders, but I was afraid to touch him. "What can I do?"

His eyes met mine and one corner of his mouth hitched. "Ask me that again later, okay?"

His gaze dipped to my breasts and left no doubt what he meant by the question. I shook my head. "You're ornery as hell. Come on. Get into the chair and I'll clean your wounds."

He stood up and I gently guided him to the nearest styling chair. His moon white hair needed a good brushing. The best I could do was pull it back into a ponytail.

I got paper towels and soaked them with warm water. As I leaned over to wipe off his ribs, Gabriel's hand snaked around my neck and pulled me close.

"I need blood, Patricia."

I looked at him, the wet paper towel poised above his skin. "I'm not a nurse, I don't do trans-fusions."

"I need to drink it."

I stared at him, my mouth agape. "Lycans don't drink blood."

"I do." He opened his mouth and needlepoint

fangs descended. He licked his lips as he leaned forward, aiming those sharp babies right at my neck.

Panic erupted. I jerked out of his grip and lurched back. "What the hell are you?"

Koschei

Translated from the Memoirs of Ruadan

After I was banished by my wife, I traveled by boat to a cold and barren place far from the land of Eire. As my new nature dictated, I drank the blood of mortal beings. In every village, I had to lie in wait for the unwary and take my sustenance by force. Soon, I gained a reputation as a *strigoi mort*—a vampire.

Word spread quickly about the *strigoi mort*. Villagers and farmers begged their gods, their wise men, and their healers for protection, but though they laid herbs on their doorsills and curses around their houses, I was not affected. Superstition was not magic—I knew real magic.

One night, I attacked a farmer, who fought so fiercely I let him go. Though I fled, I was relentlessly chased by terrified villagers. Forced to travel deeper and deeper into the craggy, snow-filled mountains, I subsisted on animal blood and slept in caves.

Three days passed. On the fourth evening, I discovered a small village tucked into the mountainside. Cold and hungry, I managed to subdue a young woman long enough to drink what I needed. But she was the favorite wife of Koschei, the dark wizard.

Koschei had a more fearsome reputation than even a *strigoi mort*. He was bone thin and wore only black robes. His hair was long and dark; his eyes as hard and green as jade. Through his magic and his psychic abilities, he coaxed from other villages food, entertainment, and companionship. Koschei had all that he needed to live a comfortable life, including many wives, concubines, and children.

I was surprised to find myself at the mercy of a mere mortal. Koschei's most powerful gift was the ability to glamour. Within moments, Koschei compelled me to tell all my secrets.

Then Koschei revealed his own secret: He was dying. He told me that he feared that his village and his family were in jeopardy; that if he died, rival peoples would attack.

"Give me immortal life and I will teach you my magic. I will show you how to draw a human to you, to drink, and to make him forget."

I agreed. What Koschei did not know was that I asked Morrigu for the ability to make others like me. She showed me the spells and the symbols for Turning. She gave me special instructions for the first six vampires I would Turn; these equals would rule the new vampire race with me.

I warned Koschei that Turning into a *deamhan fola* was risky. But I could not persuade him from his goal. We agreed that he would teach me the magic first, should the transformation fail.

Koschei spent every evening showing me the ways of the mind. He taught me how to alter his voice and how to create illusions. "People believe so easily," he said. "Show them what they expect and they will not question you."

After I learned all that I could from Koschei, I performed the ritual of Turning. I was relieved when he awoke as *deamhan fola*.

There was little time to celebrate his transformation. The next evening, his village was savagely attacked. Though Koschei and I combined our powers to fight the unknown invaders, nearly all of the villagers were slain and the buildings burned.

We escaped with three of Koschei's children deep into the mountains. Only Koschei's daughter, Ina, who was barely seventeen, survived the night.

While Koschei held vigil over his daughter, I returned to the village. I buried the dead and burned everything else to the ground. I also bespelled the area so that neither human nor beast would enter what had once been a happy place.

After the work was done and the spells cast, I returned to the cave.

Koschei was readying to leave. He knew of a powerful healer in another village. "I will take Ina to her."

We agreed to meet in one year with the other five *deamhan fola* to create a ruling Council.

Then Koschei and I parted ways.

Chapter 7

"*Patricia.*"

My name held a world of hurt. He reached one arm beseechingly toward me. I shook my head, my whole body going numb. I tossed the paper towel in the trash because I needed to do something other than look at him.

"Why do you fear me? I am no different than Lorcan or Eva or any of the other vampires who share my abilities."

"Lorcan was cured, so he's not a beast anymore. And Eva isn't a werewolf."

His eyes widened. "They didn't tell you."

I frowned, not really wanting to know what I hadn't been told.

"The cure for the Taint comes from the blood of royal lycanthropes," he said quietly. "But there is a side effect. The vampires who survive the cure retain the ability to shape-shift."

He sure sounded like he believed the malarkey coming out of his mouth. My friends would've told me the truth about something so important. Yet the werewolf side effect would explain why the Consortium hadn't released the cure to all vampires seeking it.

"Is that what happened to you?" I asked.

"No." He grimaced. "I was born with this . . . anomaly."

A lycanthrope *born* with vampire tendencies? How in the world had such a thing happened? I didn't know what to believe or how to feel. Well, okay. I was insanely attracted to Gabriel, which upset me far more than his unusual parentage. Even now, though I was scared of him, I wanted to touch him. I wanted to make him feel better. Damn. His wounds had not closed. Blood flowed onto the chair and pooled around its base.

"Why haven't you healed?" I asked.

"Demon scratches are poisonous, even to mutants such as I." His words held bitterness.

He sucked in a sharp breath and squeezed his eyes shut. "You shouldn't be alone. You're not safe."

That's right. Darrius was supposed to be watching me. Then I realized he'd probably gone off after Wilson. *Good dog.* "Why did you risk coming here again?"

His eyes flickered open. "To claim you."

"I'm not checked baggage." I put my hands on my hips and looked him over. All Gabriel needed was a little blood to help him heal. I really wanted to get closer to him—and that uncontrollable urge to be near him confused me. Terrified me.

I looked at Nonna and Dottie floating above us, hanging on to every word. "Find something else to do," I told them. For a minute, they looked as if they might protest. Nonna rolled her eyes and Dottie sighed, then *pop,* they were gone.

Uneasy, I approached Gabriel. He watched me, his expression solemn. I gripped the armrests, leaned down, and offered my neck. His lips brushed my skin. I felt electrified by that single, soft touch. Then his fangs sank into my neck and he drank.

Oh, God. My fingernails dug into the vinyl as I tried to keep my balance. Heat pulsed through me, and desire exploded. I wanted to crawl onto Gabriel's lap and devour him.

I don't remember my Turning; few of us Turn-bloods did. I couldn't recall drinking from my Master. Since then, I've never had a reason to share my blood with another vampire.

I didn't know the sensations were so erotic. Vaguely, I wondered about my donors—if they always felt this intense rush of pleasure when I drank from them. Did this terrible, aching need build within them? Was I experiencing normal reactions? Or was I responding to Gabriel?

Delicious, beautiful, dangerous Gabriel.

I couldn't stop myself. I maneuvered onto his lap, my legs dangling off the sides of the chair. I didn't care about the blood staining my jeans and shirt. I pressed closer, my hands clutching at his broad shoulders.

His hands cupped my buttocks, and he brought me against the hard-on bulging in his jeans.

I moaned. He felt so good, so right. I never wanted this moment to end.

Then it did.

"No!" I couldn't bear for him to stop. Damn it!

His fangs receded, but his lips stayed on that

spot. His tongue flicked across my neck. Lust burned bright and hot.

I cupped his face and kissed him. His lips were soft, plump. He tasted like blood and that reminded me that I hadn't eaten, either. The coppery taste inflamed me. As our tongues thrust against each other, I stroked his chest, which was smooth and firm. *He's healed!* wiggled through my fogged brain. Yay! He could do more naughty things to me.

"Patricia," he murmured. He grasped my wrists and pulled me away. "I know our destiny. I will happily mate with you, but I don't think you're ready."

Mate. Yeah. That sounded like a fine idea. I tugged my hands free and yanked the top of his jeans. The metal buttons popped off and the material parted, revealing the top of his large cock. My fingertips danced along the mushroomed head and then I caressed the sensitive ridge.

He sucked in a sharp breath. "Patricia." He let me dip my hand inside his pants, then growled in frustration. "Damn it!"

He grabbed the armrests and yanked them off. They clattered to the floor. Then he plucked me from his lap and set me on my feet. He scrambled from the chair and put his hands out in a "stop" gesture.

Someone rattled the front door of the salon. I ignored the racket and stepped toward Gabriel. His expression was caught between amusement and desperation. Blood streaked his torso and his jeans were still open. His hair had come loose again.

"You'd better answer the door," he said. "I'll hide in the bathroom."

Frustration roared through me. After he hurried into the bathroom, which was located just a few feet away in the back of the shop, I started to regain my senses. The fog of lust lifted and I felt as if I'd been released from a magic spell. Jeez. Our proximity caused me to go wild woman on him. What was wrong with me?

Rattled by my behavior and annoyed by the persistence of the unexpected customer, I turned around and marched to the door. I flicked open the bolt and the person on the other side swung into the shop.

"Why haven't you answered your cell phone?" yelled Drake.

I pushed him back through the door and shut it behind me. He looked surprised, but I wasn't about to explain why I was hiding a Consortium-wanted fugitive. Mostly because I didn't know.

"My cell phone is on." I reached into the

back pocket of my jeans and looked down at the slim device. "Oh. Well, sorry." I turned it on. "There. Problem solved. Is Darrius watching Wilson?"

"*Ja.*" Drake's nostrils flared. "What happened to your shirt?"

I looked down at my clothing. Blood from Gabriel's wounds had stained my T-shirt and jeans. "I . . . uh, cut myself. I'll go change my clothes after I'm done in the shop."

His gaze narrowed. "Is someone in there?"

"Is it your business if there is?" I asked tartly. I was relieved that Darrius was tracking Wilson, but now I was worried about protecting the other man in my life. "Can't a girl date around here?"

"Date? *You?*"

Maybe not the best lie I could've told, considering everyone knew about my ex-husband and my feelings about relationships.

I put a hand on my hip and glared at him. "Do you want something?"

"Who is the lucky man?" His jade green eyes studied my face and he grinned wickedly. "If such a thing were possible between our kind and yours, I would've asked you out a long time ago."

My mouth dropped open. As much as I flirted

with him and his brother, I'd never thunk either one of him took it seriously. He was probably yanking my chain, hoping I'd give up the identity of my new beau.

"Well, aren't you sweet, you liar." I made a shooing motion. "I got work to do and I don't want you shedding on my clean floor."

He pressed his hand against his heart. "You wound me, *Liebling*."

"Drake," I said warningly, "if you don't go away, the next time I groom you, I'll shave you bald."

He put his hands up in the air and stepped back. "I would not dream of angering my stylist. But I will be watching you, Patsy. Damian's orders."

I rolled my eyes. "Whatever. So long as you do it *outside*."

He nodded. "Deal." He walked to the concrete-block wall and leaned against it. "I'm only a scream away."

"Terrific." I returned to the shop. I looked at the closed bathroom door and pressed a hand against my roiling belly. Panic gurgled.

How the hell was I going to get Gabriel out of here?

Before I could answer my own question, the door opened. I whirled around to give Drake what for, but he wasn't the one coming into my shop.

The lady looked like Lucy Liu except she was taller and had no freckles. Her dark brown hair cascaded in thick ringlets to her ass. Jewels sparkled in the sleek strands. Her lips were bloodred and her almond-shaped eyes doe brown. The gold, knee-length dress she wore screamed *expensive* and so did the black calf boots. Gold bracelets pinged together as she sashayed past me.

As beautiful as the woman was, she carried with her a stench so bad, my eyes started watering. Hovering above her left shoulder was a black smudge. Within it were two white orbs. Ick. Eyeballs. And they were looking at me.

"We're closed," I said.

"I don't need your services," she sneered. Her delicate brow furrowed as she glanced around my shop. It wasn't fancy, but it was clean and tidy. Her arrogant glance assessed me. "You are a messy eater, my dear."

I looked down at my clothing. Blood from Gabriel's wounds had stained my T-shirt and jeans. Well, let her think I'd just devoured a donor. It wasn't any of her business.

"Like I said, we're closed. Door's this way, in

case you forgot." I hitched my thumb over my shoulder toward the front of the shop.

Her gaze landed on the closed bathroom door, and then she turned and sauntered toward me. Good God! That awful smell filled up the whole room.

The woman looked at me as though she was a scientist examining an alien. "I've found Broken Heart to be very quaint." She smiled beguilingly. "I can't believe that Lorcan and Patrick haven't already tired of their little business endeavor."

I wasn't particularly fond of the Consortium or its rules, but her condemnation got my back up. It was like picking on my sister—that was my job and no one else's.

She was obviously waiting for a response, but I didn't give her one. How many times did a person have to be told to leave? Her gaze was flat and cold. Her smile was as fake as my particle wood entertainment center. "I'm Magnolia Blossom."

"It's a shame to walk around with a name like that. I guess your parents didn't like you much."

She blinked at me, her pretty little mouth hanging open. "My real name is Hua Mu Lan. The founder of the Family Hua. I'm one of the Ancients."

"That's fantastic," I said in a tone that suggested the opposite. "Do you need shampoo or something?"

I *really* wanted her to leave. I didn't like her attitude, or the creepy thing hanging around her shoulder, or her horrible stench. If I'd had the ability to breathe, I would be running outside to gulp in fresh air. Jess had once told me that her nose had gone crazy after Turning. To this day, she said ol' Doc Michaels smelled like a ham and cheese sandwich. I wondered if I was experiencing something similar.

"Might I use your bathroom?" she asked. "I'd like to freshen up."

"The toilet's backed up," I lied. "It stinks to high heaven in there."

"Oh, I don't mind." She turned and headed toward the bathroom. Now, why did I believe she knew Gabriel was in there? And if she did, why was she looking for him?

I didn't know how to stop her, so I did the first thing that came to mind. I grabbed her shoulder and yanked her backward.

My palm felt like it had melded to her. Power zapped down my arm and surged hot and electric through my whole body.

What the hell?

Magnolia Blossom whirled around. Two

short, sharp daggers shot out from her sleeves and into her hands. She pointed them at me. As if that wasn't scary enough, flames rolled over the blades.

"Stupid little Turn-bloods like you should mind their manners."

Chapter 8

I beat a hasty retreat.

Triumph flashed in Magnolia's gaze.

"Hah! That's the pot calling the kettle black," I said angrily. "You're the rudest bitch I've ever met." I marched to the front door and pushed it open. "Don't let the door hit your ass on the way out."

I wondered if I'd signed my death warrant. In that moment, I knew she was deciding whether to kill me.

Drake entered the shop and stood close to me. His brows arched as he examined Magnolia's fiery knives. "Is there a problem, Lia?"

"No. I was merely showing Patsy my newest weapons." She blew out the flames and sheathed them. She strode to the doorway and paused on the threshold.

"Never lay your hands on me again," she warned softly.

"Don't come within throttling distance and I won't."

Her eyes flashed with hatred. Then she stomped out, taking the stench and the entity with her. Whew. I was glad she was gone. I locked up again and leaned against the door. Man, I was feeling dizzy.

Drake grinned. "You sure know how to make friends."

"It's a talent."

He studied me, his gaze worried. "Patricia—"

"I know, I know," I said. "I should show more respect to the Ancients. But I don't care who you are. If you act like an asshole, then I'm treating you like one."

"I would never tell you how to behave," said Drake, chuckling. He sobered, eyeing me with a frown. "Let's go see what's in the bathroom, shall we?"

"Drake!"

He strode across the room and flung the door open.

The bathroom was empty.

I turned away to hide my surprise and relief. I didn't want Drake reading my expression.

"It's not backed up," he said. "Why did you lie to Lia?"

I didn't bother to ask how he'd know that. Listening at the door with his big wolfie ears.

"I wanted her to leave. I don't like her." I hurried to the hair care display and started rearranging it.

"Was he in there?"

Drake's voice was so close, it startled me. I dropped the Paul Mitchell Awapuhi shampoo. I glanced over my shoulder and saw Drake less than a foot away. I met my friend's suspicious gaze.

"Who?" I asked.

"Your new boyfriend."

"None of your beeswax."

"C'mon, Patsy. Who is he?"

"A troll named Wolf Eater." I pointed to the door. "Go away."

"Torturing you is more fun."

I put the shampoo down. "I'm going to my trailer to take a shower and change my clothes. You are going outside."

"All right, all right!" He put his hands up, palms out in a gesture of surrender. "I'll walk you to the trailer and stand guard on your porch."

His cell phone buzzed. He unclipped it and answered. He listened for a moment, then said, "Okay. Be right there."

"Wilson?"

"Promise me that you'll stay in the trailer until I return."

"Fine," I said. I locked up the shop and hurried across the weed-choked field. I stood on the second step, looking down at Drake. He turned away and I reached out and snagged his shoulder. "Stay safe," I said.

"If I do, will you give me a full-body shampoo?"

I laughed. "On the house."

He grinned; then he scurried away, off to whatever emergency required his attention.

When I entered the trailer, I noticed two things. One, my couch had been covered by a big, red blanket, probably because of the bloodstains. And two, the white wolf was sitting on it, his big tongue lolling out of his mouth.

"Hey!" I said crossly. "No dogs on the furniture!"

He woofed and jumped off, then padded around the coffee table to sit by my feet. "God, you're cute."

I pushed off from the door and stumbled. The room started to spin. Darkness crimped the edges of my vision. I heard the wolf bark, and then I was falling, falling into oblivion.

"You sucked her dry," said an irritated female voice. I floated on the edge of consciousness, hearing the conversation, but was too tired to open my eyes. Exhaustion felt like concrete blocks pressing down on me.

"I didn't know she hadn't eaten yet." Gabriel sounded worried and defensive. "I didn't mean to take so much. She . . . we . . . um, *she* . . . oh, just give her the blood!"

"All right. I'll be her dinner this once. But you'd better be careful, Gabriel."

"You know how it is with the mating lust, even for me. When a lycan meets his mate, it's . . . powerful. Even she could not resist."

"Just remember that mating lust overpowers even the strongest alpha. You might not be able to stop next time."

"I hope I will not have to stop."

"Ew. Please. I don't want to hear the details."

The velvet skin of a wrist was pressed against my mouth. My fangs reacted immediately, piercing the delicate flesh. The blood that flowed into my mouth tasted like nirvana. I drank until I was full.

Then their voices faded into the ether and I floated once more.

I awoke on the couch in my trailer, feeling better, if not a little groggy. I looked at the wall clock. It was a little after midnight. I felt as though I'd slept for a week.

It was obvious that I was alone in the trailer. "Wilson?" I called.

No answer. His music wasn't blasting, which was a bad sign. If the boy was home, his tunes were on. Why hadn't Darrius brought him home?

Well, I'd just call Darrius and find out. Wilson had a few friends in town, but mostly he skulked around, finding hidey-holes and places to drink and drug.

I sat up and stretched.

Where had Gabriel gone? He'd been here earlier with someone else. He was the reason I'd gotten breakfast. Who'd been my donor?

My clothes had been changed. I wore a pink baby doll shirt that said in glittery gold sparkles: COUNTRY MUSIC STAR. I also wore jeans and pink ankle socks. My boots sat next to the couch.

My gaze fell on a Post-it note left on the coffee table.

Stay here. Will return soon.
Love,
G.

Oooo, I had the warm fuzzies. It was silly to feel mushy about a simple note, but he'd cared enough to leave it.

I was worried about Wilson. I reached for my address book on the end table, then grabbed the mobile phone.

Someone knocked.

"Who is it?" I called out as I hurried to the door. My heart tripped over in my chest. Was it Wilson? Or Gabriel? I was surprised at how much I wanted to see that ornery fugitive again.

"My name is Terran," said a female voice. "Gabriel sent me."

Warily, I clenched the handle. "No offense, but how can I trust you?"

"Because I could easily rip off the door or bust through the wall."

Trepidation squeezed me, but I unlocked the door and opened it.

The woman was thin, wiry. She barely reached my chin. She would've been beautiful if the left side of her face had not had a long, jagged scar puckering the skin. Her black hair was pulled into a ponytail.

She wore a bomber jacket, skintight jeans, and biker boots that buckled on the side. She carried a half sword that was smooth-sharp on one side and wicked-jagged on the other. In the belt around her waist were small knives and on her left hip, a 9mm.

Jeez. Talk about being prepared for the worst. Her brown gaze assessed me. Then she bent down on one knee and lowered her head. "My queen."

For a full minute, I gaped at Terran. Me, a queen? Was she kidding? Huh. She seemed serious about her homage. And here I thought tonight couldn't get any weirder.

"Honey, I'm the best beautician in these parts, but I ain't the queen of hair care."

She rose to her feet. I moved aside to let her in; then I shut the door.

"You're very funny. Humor is a good quality in a leader."

Riiiight. "Where's Gabriel?"

She paced the small living room, her gaze darting all over the place. "He'll return soon."

"Are you a . . . er, hybrid, too?"

"Hmph. I suppose hybrid is a better word

than mutant. Or abomination." She shrugged. "I'm your garden-variety lycan. Only Gabriel is *loup de sang*."

"Loop de what?"

"*Loup de sang.* Blood wolf."

"Oh." God, she was making me nervous with her pacing and constant checking of the windows. "I've been taking care of myself for a while now. I don't need a babysitter."

"It is my honor to serve you, my queen."

"I'm *not* a queen."

"You will rule the vampires and the werewolves." Her gaze pinned mine. "The Vederes are never wrong."

"Who the hell are the Vederes?"

"A family of prophets. Astria Vedere predicted that one of the Broken Heart Turn-bloods would rule the two nations."

Choo-choo. Train to Loonyville departing the station.

"You have the wrong Turn-blood, honey." I walked to the couch and sat down. Terran refused my offer of a chair. She went to the window and peered out.

"What are you guys doing in Broken Heart? And why are you hiding from the Consortium?"

Terran's gaze flicked to me. "These are questions Gabriel should answer."

"Well, he's not here and you are."

She moved back from the window. "We're hunted by everyone. Lycans, vampires, the Roma. We are not welcome anywhere." She stood near the couch, arms crossed. "Except maybe here. We heard about the vampire-lycans who roam free. It is said that anyone who seeks safety and a new life can find it in Broken Heart."

I was fuzzy on the Consortium's plans for the town. Something about being one of the first communities where parakind could settle down and live openly. It hadn't occurred to me how many non-humans were looking for a place to hang their hats.

Terran cocked her head. "You have visitors. I'll sneak out the window in your bedroom." She plucked a knife and the gun from her waist-band arsenal and put them on the coffee table. "In case you need them, Queen Patricia."

I rolled my eyes. I didn't understand anything that had happened today. I must've somehow entered an alternate reality. Queens and new kinds of vampires and crazy lycans—jeez! The world had gone mad.

Terran strode through the kitchen and into my bedroom. She closed the door softly behind her. I put on my boots and tucked the little knife inside one. Then I grabbed the gun, hurried into the kitchen, and threw it into the freezer.

I opened the door after the first knock.

Patrick and Jessica greeted me. I saw how they were looking at me. With pity. With certainty. Foreboding slid into my stomach and sat there like a hot brick. I knew it could be only one thing.

They couldn't be here to tell me . . . oh, God. The word escaped on a sob. "Wilson?"

Chapter 9

"Calm yourself," said Patrick. His smooth Irish voice slid over me and my panic receded. I vaguely realized he'd used glamour on me, but I didn't care. "Let's sit down, Patsy."

Zombielike, I moved backward, turning and walking to my couch. I sat woodenly, feeling as though my whole world were falling apart. Patrick and Jessica joined me on the couch, but I couldn't look at them. I couldn't bear all their sympathy.

"We found Wilson's backpack," said Patrick.

"Backpack?" I didn't understand. Had he decided to go to school?

"It had some clothes, his iPod, and money," said Jessica.

It took me only a second to figure out the significance of those contents. My useless, dead heart dropped like a stone.

"You mean he was running away?" Horror filled me like acid, burning my insides to a crisp. Anguish forced me to cover my face, to suck in unnecessary breaths. I balled up the pain, tucking it into a corner of my mind so I could take it out later and deal with it.

"So, he's missing, right?" I asked. "You're not saying he's—he's dead."

"He's not dead," said Patrick. "Darrius was attacked by Andhaka. Darrius is okay, but by the time he escaped, Wil was gone. Damian tracked down the backpack. He lost Wil's scent in the woods."

How the hell did a werewolf lose a scent? My son was out there with demons and Wraiths and God knew what else. Why did I let him go out? I should've duct taped him to his bed.

"Things are getting too dangerous," said Jessica. "We're moving everyone into the compound."

"No." I shook my head. "I'm not leaving my house. Wil might come back."

"It's for the best." Jessica reached over and

grasped my shoulder. "We'll station a guardian nearby and—"

"No."

Patrick leaned forward and stared at me. "You *will*—"

"Don't you dare try to glamour me again!" Fury raced through me. I felt the heat of that anger pulse in my veins. I rose up on shaky legs and pointed a finger at Patrick. "The Consortium does not run my life!"

Fire shot out of my fingertip. Patrick dodged and the flame hit the lamp shade on the end table. Before I could utter, "Oh, shit," Patrick had gotten a glass of water from the kitchen. He dumped it on the burning shade.

"How did you do that?" he asked, his eyes wide. "It's not your Family power."

"I—I don't know." I examined my fingertip. It wasn't singed or anything. Had touching Magnolia Blossom earlier temporarily transferred her power to me? Ack! I had touched Durga, too, and felt the same fiery power surge. "It's a fluke, that's all."

"Some fluke," said Jessica. She stared at me, frowning. Then she shook her head. "Patsy," she pleaded, "moving into the compound really is the safest option."

"We aren't ever gonna be safe, for the love of

God! All the Ancients are here, Jess. Of course, Koschei is gonna attack us now." I stared at my friend. My anger gave way to shock. I pointed my finger at Jess and she ducked.

"Don't do that!" she said. "I don't want to get fried."

I shook my finger, then flicked it. "See? It's out. No more fire." I turned my gaze to Patrick. "You brought the Ancients here on purpose, didn't you?"

"Stay here if you like," said Patrick a little too quickly. "Drake is leading the team searching for Wilson."

That information made me feel better. At least someone at the Consortium gave a shit about us. I softened toward Patrick. However, Jessica had been chewing on my comment and she turned to her husband. "You're setting a trap. And you didn't fucking tell me."

"I tell you everything."

"The hell you do!"

I backed away until I was safe in the kitchen. Jess in full rant was something to see, I'll tell you.

Patrick had been married to her long enough to know when to retreat. He gripped her by the arms, probably to prevent her from whipping out her swords. Gold sparkles showered my living room as they popped out of sight.

I crossed my arms and thought about what to do next. Joining the search for Wilson seemed like the motherly thing to do, but damn it, I couldn't find him any better than the wolfies. They had all the skills and talents I lacked. The best thing I could do was stick close to the house in case he came back.

Oh, Wilson. Did he dump his stuff and take off? Had someone attacked him and dragged him away? I pressed a hand against my roiling stomach. *Please, God,* I begged, *don't let anything happen to him.*

I didn't much expect God to be listening, but I wasn't taking any chances. I just wanted Wilson to be all right.

My mind wouldn't let go of the last conversation I had with my son. *We had that stupid fight and I didn't tell him I loved him and oh, God, where is he?*

My son hated for me to go near his room. I felt like a sneak-thief as I opened the door and stepped inside. It smelled like pot and incense.

I sat on his bed and stared at the posters on his walls. I didn't recognize any of the bands. Of course, he liked heavy metal stuff, which just sounded like a bunch of yelling and clanging to me. I loved country music, which drove Wilson up the wall.

"Hey, Mom, what do you get when you play country music backward?"

"I don't know," I said, grinning.

"You get your truck back, your dog back, your wife back, your beer back. . . ."

I laughed at the memory. It had been a long time since we'd been that easy with each other. My gaze returned to the posters.

I supposed that pretty much summed up our relationship. He was rock'n'roll and I was country.

Restless and worried, I wandered into the living room and plopped onto the couch. I remembered how many times Sean sat on this very sofa, weeping like a man wanting to repent. Yeah, he wept like a baby and my heart broke for him. For us. For Wilson.

I won't do it anymore. I'll go to the meetings, Patsy. I love you. You and Willie are my family. I can't do this alone. I need you, honey. I need your support. Please.

Tears. Promises. Lies.

Alcoholics were penitent. They meant what they said; at least they did when they said it. They just didn't have the follow-through. The alcohol was stronger than their willpower, their ability to love themselves or their families, their need to be decent human beings. They forgot important family events, they spent money meant for bills, and they drove cars while intoxicated. They passed out in ditches, in lawn chairs, in recliners. They got put in jail. In outreach programs. In facilities with doctors and psychiatrists.

I went to meetings, too. I learned that alcoholism was a disease and that Sean didn't choose to be an alcoholic.

But Sean sure as hell didn't choose to be sober, either. I learned to focus on myself and my kid. To stop worrying about Sean, to stop pouring alcohol down the sink, to stop putting a pillow under his head when he passed out on the floor.

Sean was always in pain. He always felt sad and guilty and needy. *I love you. Give me another chance.*

Then the day came when I was all out of second chances. I hoped to God I wouldn't have to make the same decision with my son. Wilson had already started on the same path as his daddy.

I picked up the remote and turned on the television. Nothing on the TV interested me, but I kept flipping through the channels.

"Hey, I like that Alton Brown," said Nonna.

I screamed and dropped the remote. My grandmother was sitting right next to me, staring at the Food Network. I wanted to throttle her.

"People are constantly sneaking up on you," said Dottie, who sat in the chair to the right. "You kinda suck as a vampire." She cackled at her own joke.

"Wilson's missing," I announced.

This news didn't much ping on their radars. Nonna was mesmerized by Mr. Brown's take on making homemade ice cream. "Just where the hell have you two been?"

"Around," said Nonna. "Don't worry about your boy, Patsy. He's all right."

I wanted to believe her, but why should I? Ghosts didn't necessarily mark the difference between alive and dead. "You two could be more useful. You're ghosts. You can go anywhere. It'd be easy for you to track him down."

"Leave it be, child," chided my grandmother. Her eyes never left the TV. "Now, ssshhh!"

"I can't stand this," I said. "I'm going to open up the shop and . . . and . . . clean it."

"There's no point to doing that," said Nonna.

Oh, here we go. Nonna had let it be known even before she died that she didn't appreciate my hairstyling techniques or my business sense.

"Why not?" I scooped up the TV remote, but stopped just short of whapping her ghostly skull. "Because I don't have many clients? Because I'm not good at my job? Because I shouldn't touch people's scalps now that I'm undead?"

"Nope," said my grandmother, unperturbed by my sarcasm. "You can't go to the shop because it's on fire."

Hua Mu Lan

Translated from the Memoirs of Ruadan

Hua Mu Lan translates loosely to "Magnolia Blossom."

But Lia was no delicate flower. A skilled warrior with the supernatural ability to wield fire, she was always ready for a fight. In the early days, I found her temperament sexy enough to do a hundred-year binding with her—twice. Over time, her battle-prone attitude became wearisome.

All the same, Lia embraced life with a fierceness I admired.

I traveled for a while after leaving Koschei. One evening, I came upon a battleground in the lands that would later be known as China. Soldiers lay upon the blood-soaked ground like chaffs of wheat cut down and tossed about. As I found a path around the carnage, I heard the soft moans of one dying.

She had taken off her helmet and dragged herself between two large rocks. Given the severity of her wounds, I knew it wouldn't be too much longer before she died.

With dirt smudging her cheek, her dark eyes alight with determination, she faced me down. The almond shape of her eyes softened the intensity of her obsidian gaze. Energy pulsed around her. Cupping her hands, she created a ball of fire.

I knew then she would be a magnificent vampire.

I made her the offer, warned her of the risks, but she was already an unconventional woman. She had disguised herself as a man to join the army—to protect her ill and aged father from conscription.

As the centuries passed, I always wondered if Lia had made up this story to satisfy those who looked no deeper for her motives. She rarely exhibited the kindness and self-sacrifice so often attributed to the heroine in the "Ballad of Mulan."

The Turning was successful and after traveling together for a while, Lia claimed she had matters to take care of.

Years passed before I learned that Lia had a young daughter. About the time I tracked down my own sons and Turned them, Lia did the same. Unlike the other Ancients with blood children Turned, she never revealed her daughter's name or location.

But that was later. Before we went our separate ways, Lia agreed to meet with me and Koschei and take her place among the Council of *deamhan fola.*

Chapter 10

"*What?*" My stupid vampire senses kicked in about that time. I smelled the smoke and heard the crackling flames even before I burst through the door and jumped over the stairs.

Helpless, I stood in the field between my trailer and my beauty shop, and watched the business my grandparents built go up in flames.

"Where is everyone?" I screamed.

No wolfies. The guardians of vampires and of Broken Heart weren't around, not anywhere. So much for the extra protection that had been promised.

I stared at the flames, clenching my fists. Had the demon returned to destroy my beauty shop?

Nonna and Dottie stood next to me. I turned to my grandmother. "Who did this?"

"I dunno." She looked at me. "I never said you weren't a good hairstylist, honey."

The dead had different priorities. I had noticed that at moments when it felt like my life was falling apart, neither Nonna nor Dottie seemed to give a ripe shit. This was the business that Nonna and Poppa had built with their own hands, but she wasn't the least bit upset. And yet, if I had the ability to shed tears, I would have. I fell to my knees and dry-wept.

I didn't realize how bright the flames were or how my body was reacting to the raging light. My first clue was the pain shimmering up my thighs. I dropped my hands from my face and stared stupidly at the wisps of smoke rising from my arms.

Only then did I realize that my skin was sizzling. Pain throbbed in every part of me that was exposed to the fire.

"Patricia!"

I looked up and saw Gabriel running toward me. He scooped me into his arms and ran toward the forest. Relief cascaded through me. He was all right. I hadn't realized how worried I'd been. I thought he'd . . . abandoned me. How stupid to have those kinds of expectations of someone I'd just met.

Every jouncing step brought fresh waves of pain, but I was damned glad to be getting away from the fire. I was gladder to be in the arms of Gabriel.

"My house is over there," I pointed out as he ran past it. As he hurried toward the protection of the trees, I stared over his shoulder. A ball of fire shot from the sky and engulfed my trailer.

"Shit!" I screamed.

I watched the flames attack my home with greedy red fingers. Then we entered the tree line and I couldn't see the carnage anymore.

A few minutes later, Gabriel skidded to a stop and laid me on the ground. "I didn't think I was going to make it in time."

"In time for what?" I asked vaguely. Away from the fire, my body had stopped smoking. But my skin was raw and blackened. I felt strange, as if I weren't quite connected to my own body. Everything felt distant. "A fireball blew up my house. Isn't that weird?"

"Drink from me, Patsy." He exposed his neck to me. Oh, he looked delicious. I sank my fangs into his carotid artery and drank. I grabbed onto his shirt and moaned, sucking in that yummy blood. I swear my body went up a thousand degrees. I was burning again, but not because of the fire.

"Sweetheart," he murmured. He disengaged my mouth from his neck and sat back to look at me.

"Why do I feel like jumping your bones every time I get within three feet of you?" I asked.

"I have that effect on a lot of women."

I bopped him on the shoulder. Then I leaned against a tree and closed my eyes, letting the blood do its work. I felt his fingers drift across my cheek. When the pain dissipated and I felt normal again, I opened my eyes and found his face inches from mine. Concern was evident in his golden gaze.

"What the hell is going on?" I asked.

"Someone wants you dead."

"I'm already dead." I took a shuddering breath. "Wilson."

For once, I was grateful for my son's sneaky ways. If he had been in there when the trailer blew up . . . oh, God! I tried to stand, but Gabriel pushed me back down.

"I found your son. He's safe."

I stared at him, dumbfounded.

"We monitor the guardians' radio transmissions. Terran heard the call go out." Regret flickered in his eyes. "I had hoped to find your son before you realized he intended to run away."

The warm fuzzies attacked me again, but they didn't just flutter in my belly. They crept up and wedged into my heart. He'd gone to find my son. He hadn't wanted me to worry. He had tried to take care of *me*. I didn't know how to feel about that. I had never been taken care of before. It seemed like I was always the one in charge, carrying the burden of the whole family, making sure everything got done.

Thanks to Gabriel, my son was okay.

Me, on the other hand . . .

"Why would someone try to off me? I'm a beautician, for God's sake. I'm nobody."

"That's not true."

I stared at him. My gaze dipped to the cream shirt that so finely molded his muscled chest. "I really want to lick you."

"I know." He smiled. He was so gorgeous. I couldn't believe I was breathing the same air as he was. He seemed otherworldly—I mean more so than most vampires. I wanted to run my fingers through his hair and cup that strong jaw, and press my lips against the pulse beating in his throat.

"All the Broken Heart Turn-bloods have been targeted," said Gabriel. "Three others were attacked, but luckily escaped. Everyone, except you, has vacated to the compound."

"I suppose that information came over the airwaves, too?"

He nodded.

"Why would anyone want any of us dead?"

"The Vedere prophecy," he said softly. "One among you will unite the vampires and lycanthropes."

"Yeah. Terran seems to think it's me."

"It is, Patricia."

"Gabriel!" Terran's voice was full of irritation. "Let's go!" She hurried toward us. "My queen," she said, dropping to one knee. "I'm sorry I failed you."

"I'll let it go this time," I said drolly. The poor child was delusional if she thought I was some kind of royalty. Hell, they all were.

Her lips quirked, but she stalled the grin. She popped to her feet, glaring at Gabriel. Whatever respect, however misplaced, she had for me didn't seem to extend to him. She pointed her sword at him. "Can we go, already? Or shall we wait around for another barrage of fire?"

"Terran believes she's in charge of me," explained Gabriel as he helped me to my feet.

"Move it!" barked Terran. She waved us forward, and we went. She walked behind us, the sword ready in her hand. I sure wouldn't mess with her.

I had no idea where we were going. But we weren't the only ones going there. Nonna and Dottie drifted along right next to us. Dottie was smoking, too. Bitch. She gave Terran the once-over. "Not much you can do about that scar, but she's got fabulous hair."

"I always wanted a sword," said Nonna as she poked her finger through Terran's blade. "How much do you think it weighs?"

"You didn't have the strength to pull a slot handle," I scoffed. "How do you expect to swing around a sword?"

"I can swing it quite well, I assure you." Terran sounded miffed.

Oh, yeah. I forgot that not everyone knew about my gift. Most people weren't real thrilled to know that ghosts were hanging around, much less that I could converse with them.

"Remember, Terran? Patricia speaks to the dead," said Gabriel proudly. Hmm. How had he known that?

"There are ghosts around us?" she asked.

"I'm talking to my grandma." I glanced over my shoulder. Terran looked way too tense, which made *me* tense. "She likes your sword."

"Terrific."

She'd barely gotten the word out when Gabriel stopped and jerked me behind him.

Then I heard the burning whine of another fireball. I looked up and nearly wet myself.

The fire exploded right in front of us. The trees lit up instantly.

"This way!" screamed Terran. She turned around and went to the left, taking another route to wherever the hell we were going. If I had a heartbeat, it would've been pounding furiously. Even so, I felt as scared as I ever had in my life. I still didn't understand what was happening or why.

I didn't have much time to think about it. Terran slashed away at the tangled brush, while Gabriel held my hand tightly and kept me close. I smelled the burning trees and heard the crackle of falling branches. Who—or what—was lobbing fire at us?

"Where are we going?" I shouted. Like it mattered. Because anywhere had to be safer than here.

Terran stopped so suddenly, I plowed into her. She didn't budge. Instead, she leaned down, muttered some pretty-sounding words, and pulled on the ground.

An earth-covered door popped open. "Go, my queen."

I wasn't about to argue, so I skittered into the dark hole. I slid down the slimy tunnel until my feet hit a stone floor. I staggered forward, righting myself, and looked around.

I was in a low-lit cave. I couldn't figure out where the source of light was coming from, but I was glad it wasn't pitch-black.

Gabriel arrived next, landing on his feet in a much more graceful manner, and then Terran jumped out of the hole. She worked some more juju on the opening and it melted away, leaving only the bumpy rock of the cave wall.

I had seen some seriously weird things since I became a vampire, but even I was impressed with Terran's magical abilities.

"Keep moving." Terran charged left, down the dimly lit corridor and once again, we followed her. Our little journey ended when she darted into a large cavern, lit by hundreds of white orbs floating around the ceiling. Huh. I thought only the Family Ruadan could create fairy lights.

In here, it didn't look much like a cave. The floor was smooth, though the walls still retained their craggy shapes. A large, white marble fountain sat in the center of the room. In the middle was the statue of a woman in a flowing gown. Her hair was swept into an updo and her face held a pensive expression. She looked familiar, but I couldn't quite place where I'd seen the face.

The woman stood next to a large wolf. One hand was on the head of the animal and the other held a crystal orb. It was from this that water flowed into the surrounding pool.

Around the fountain were various chaises and settees in bold colors. A girl with shockingly pink hair and paper white skin lounged on a yellow couch. She was wearing pajamas the color of her hair. Piled around her and her seat were dusty, thick books. She didn't look up from perusing the large book open on her lap.

One section seemed to have beds, and another part was filled with all kinds of computers and other gadgets. In the far right corner was a large desk covered by files, loose papers, books, and food debris. There were other people, too, in the shadows and on the sidelines who were waiting, watching.

Pink Hair gave me the once-over, looking none too impressed. "*She's* your queen?" she asked, her British accent thick. "Is that your real hair color?"

"Is that yours?" I retorted, turning away from her. "Where's Wilson?" I asked Gabriel. "You said he was safe."

"That foul-mouthed brat was yours, was he?" said Pink Hair. She lazily turned another page. "Zipped 'is mouth up, I did. Put him in the dungeon, too."

My vampire speed came in real handy. I enjoyed the look of surprise on the girl's face when she found herself dangling from my hand, my fingers squeezing her throat. Her eyes were pink, too. That kinda freaked me out, but I didn't let go.

I stared into her pink eyes. "Get. My. Son."

Chapter 11

"Once again, Zerina, you've done a fab job of pissing off the wrong people." Terran sighed as she sheathed her sword.

Zerina couldn't say much, seeing as how I was squeezing the breath out of her. Gabriel laid a hand on my arm. My skin tingled at the contact.

"Zee isn't the most tactful person, but we like having her around."

"I won't ask you twice." I dropped her bony ass onto the chaise and she scrambled off it. I got the distinct impression she was both shocked and pissed off, but I didn't care. I watched her hurry toward a dark tunnel a few feet away.

"She's a fairy. Glamour doesn't work on her," Gabriel said.

"Yeah, well, fear seemed to do the trick." If he thought I gave a crap about Zerina being a fairy, he was wrong.

Nerve-wracked, I turned and studied the fountain. Man alive, I just knew I'd seen that woman before. Had it been as a human or as a vampire? I'd never been normal, not even as a human being, much as I tried. As a vampire, I'd pretty much left normal behind for good. I slept through the day and drank blood and could see ghosts.

I heard footsteps and turned. Wilson exited the tunnel, followed by Zerina. She shot me a look of pure pissed off, but I didn't care. Relief cascaded through me as I hurried toward Wilson with every intention of yanking him into my arms.

He avoided the embrace.

He seemed relieved to see me, but he couldn't stop resenting me long enough to just hug me. Hurt crowded my chest, but I tried not to show it.

Zerina smirked. "He ain't got no respect for no one, has he? Not even the only one here who loves 'im. Arsehole."

She practically skipped back to her chaise and her books. I almost followed and throttled her right then and there because doing so would be easier than admitting she was right.

Wilson didn't respect me. He was too caught up in his own fears and failures to try to see beyond his world and into mine. He was punishing me for his childhood, for his dad's leaving, for my staying—hell, I had a whole list of sins to pay for. Some weren't even mine, but I felt the weight of the guilt. I took the penalties.

Isn't that what you did when you loved someone more than your ownself?

"Thanks for saving my son," I said, hearing the catch in my own voice. "How do we get out of here?"

"You must stay with us. It is our duty to protect you," said Terran. Zerina snorted at this proclamation, but one look from Gabriel shut her up.

"You are the foretold ruler," he said.

"Why don't you tell her the rest," goaded Zerina.

"For the love of God!" I wheeled around and glared at him. The people who had not yet revealed themselves backed up into the shadows. "Cut the crap, all right? I don't know what kind of game you're playing, but I'm out."

"Huh. She doesn't strike me as queenly," said Zerina.

"That's enough, Zee," snapped Gabriel. "She is the one named by the prophecy."

Oh, here we go again! I looked at Gabriel. "Y'know, I don't understand anything that's gone on since the day we met."

Wilson flopped onto one of the empty couches. He stared moodily at the fountain, pretending not to care. But he was listening. He was storing up every word spoken. I imagine he would have plenty to say about me and Gabriel.

Zerina extracted a book from her pile. The cover sported a big, black wolf howling up at the moon. The title was *Werewolves Are Real!* by Theodora Maribelle Monroe.

Brows raised, I looked at her.

"Page twenty-three," she said. "It's bookmarked."

I took the werewolf book and thumbed through the pages until I got to the right page. I read:

Legend of the *Loup de Sang*

In 1807, a small group of *loup-garou* immigrated from France to the town of Vincennes, the capital city in Indian Territory. In nine years, the area would become Indiana, the nineteenth state admitted to the Union.

Among the new arrivals was the widow Chantelle Marchand, who was eight months pregnant. Destitute and in need of protection from those who'd killed her husband, Chantelle made the long, treacherous journey to the United States to live with her father, Jacques Marchand.

Several years earlier, Marchand had come to the States and been among the first French traders to settle the area. He was the alpha of the local pack, and lived with his people in a community outside Vincennes.

Not long after Chantelle arrived, a territorial dispute erupted among the *loup-garou* and the *deamhan fola*, or vampires (read more about these creatures in my book: *Vampires Are Real!*).

One evening, the vampires viciously attacked the werewolves. The battle was intense and gruesome.

Chantelle was among the casualties.

As she lay dying, her father delivered a boy, whom they called Gabriel. Fortunately, Chantelle was able to see her son moments before she passed from the earthly plane.

However, the newborn had been affected by the vampire's attack on his mother.

Translated from the diary of Jacques Marchand:

I write these words with a heavy heart. My beloved Chantelle is dead, but the child I cut from her womb lives.

He is an abomination. Yet I cannot bring myself to rid the world of this creature. It is the fault of the vampires. They took my daughter's life and cursed my grandchild.

Gabriel will not take milk. It is only by accident that I discovered his true sustenance: blood. He sleeps all day and stays up all night. Sunlight hurts him. Yet his heart beats. And he breathes.

The vampire who killed Chantelle tried to Turn her. I know the laws of the Ancients: No vampire will feed upon the flesh of lycanthropes, nor mate with them, nor Turn them.

By the time I arrived, the poison of the deamhan fola *raced in my daughter's veins. Killing him so quickly was a mistake. He should've suffered for his sins.*

Already whispers and rumors run through the pack about my grandchild, the loup de sang. *Soon, they will call a Council and de-*

*mand action. I am the alpha. I must do what is
best for the pack.*

Marchand never again wrote about his
grandchild, whom he called *loup de sang*, or
blood wolf. To this day, rumors abound
about Gabriel. Given that most werewolves
live into their eight hundreds (and who
knows how long *loup de sang* lived!),
Gabriel is in the prime of his life.

That is, if his grandfather did not kill
him.

I looked at Gabriel. "Is this true?"

"Yes. It's just like I told you before, Patricia. I
was born into both worlds. And yet, I am not
part of either one."

I shut the book. I couldn't imagine running
for your lives for two hundred years. I wondered how Arin and Terran got hooked up with
him. Not to mention Zerina. How did you bring
an irritable fairy into a lycanthrope family?

I thought I'd gotten a raw deal getting Turned
into a vampire, but Gabriel had been born one.
It was one thing to have your life irrevocably
changed and quite another to have a life you
couldn't change.

"And this prophecy everyone keeps going on about?"

Gabriel opened his mouth to answer, but the words that echoed into the cave were not his.

"What the bloody hell have you done?" The shouted accusation arrived about five seconds before the man did. He appeared in a poof of white smoke. He was tall and thin, wearing a black robe with gold edging. The hood was thrown back. His hair was gray and shaggy, his face pockmarked and wrinkled. I couldn't begin to guess his age, but he was old. His dark brown eyes took in the surroundings, landing on me last.

"Patricia! We thought you were. . ."

"Dead?" supplied Zerina in a tone suggesting she wished that were the case.

The man stalked toward Gabriel, waving his toothpick arms. "What were you thinking, boy? I told you not to go back."

His gold eyes flashed with anger. "You know I cannot leave my mate in danger, Arin." He brushed a loose curl away from my cheek. "I returned to you, Patricia. I recall you were rather happy to see me."

That little reminder made me shut up.

Arin turned to Gabriel. "We must stay the course. No more going off on your own."

"I'll go wherever I like," said Gabriel. "Especially if Patricia needs me."

The man sighed as he walked between the couches and looked at Wilson. "*Who* is this?"

"The queen's son," answered Zerina. "Guess that makes him the prince."

Wilson's eyes widened as he chewed on that thought.

I stepped between the men, my gaze on the new guy. "Don't fill his head up with ideas," I said. "What's going on? Who are you?"

"My name is Arin," he said. "Terran is my daughter. And I've known this arrogant whelp all his life."

Gabriel growled. I blinked up at him. He looked as fierce as he did in his wolf form. "We do not have time for games. Our plan did not take into account the Ancients' war."

Arin sighed. "You can't simply walk up to an unsuspecting Turn-blood, announce that she is savior of two peoples, and expect her to rejoice."

"Thank *you*," I said. Then I frowned. "What?"

Gabriel's agitation was palpable. "They hid Lorcan's condition from everyone. I have been shunned since birth, but the Consortium mutants enjoy freedom and respect!"

"Patience is a quality you have to yet cultivate, boy. The prophecy is on the cusp of coming true. But you cannot force it. Given your impudence, you might well have delayed it."

What was this crapola? Mostly the Consortium did whatever it wanted and I didn't give a rat's ass as long as I got to keep my way of life. But what little had been left of my life was gone. The sudden realization that I would never walk back into my beauty shop buckled my knees.

Gabriel wrapped his arm around me and drew me into his embrace. I let him do it. I hadn't wanted to think about why I felt so connected to him.

"Hua Mu Lan has turned against the Ancients," said Terran. "She's joined with Koschei."

Arin swung away from us and paced in front of the fountain. "Lia is impetuous and enjoys her power. It is not surprising she would align with Koschei."

"Wait a minute. That snotty bitch with the stupid name blew up my house?" I couldn't wrap my brain around this idea. What about that horrid little apparition hanging around her and that god awful stench? "She stinks."

"That's a mild way of putting it," said Terran.

"No, I mean it literally. My friend Jessica said that François smelled like garbage." I received blank looks. "He's the vampire who tried to kill Jess a few months back. Anyway, she was the only one who noticed the stench. And he had the Taint."

Everyone in the room stared at me. Oh, hell. Why had I opened my big mouth? Now, wait a minute. If the smell was attached to the ugly spirit, then it made sense that I was the only one who'd noticed it.

"She had a nasty ghost pet," I offered. "Maybe that thing was what stank to high heaven."

"What did it look like?" asked Arin.

"A big black spot with two white marble-looking eyes."

"Definitely not a ghost." Arin walked to the desk and started digging through a pile of books. "I didn't realize you also had the ability to see demon spirits."

"Me, either." I didn't want to see demons. Hell, I didn't want to see ghosts. I couldn't help but think about how I'd touched Durga—and maybe that was why I saw the demon hanging around Lia. Then I'd touched Lia and almost set Patrick's hair on fire.

"The demon attacking the Turn-bloods is Durga's pet," I said. "We had a run-in earlier."

"Koschei's recruited one more Ancient to his

cause," said Zerina. She sounded utterly delighted at the prospect. It made me wonder what sins the Ancients had committed against her.

"If that's so," said Arin gravely, "we are in for a bigger battle than I feared."

Chapter 12

I pulled out of Gabriel's grip, then walked to a nearby couch and dropped into it. "I feel like I've been cast in an episode of *Supernatural*."

"We have a lot to explain," said Arin. He had abandoned his search for whatever demon-related information he'd wanted.

"Why don't you start with the prophecy and go from there?" I asked.

I wasn't sure how to feel. I was really good at shoving down my emotions, but the information being lobbed at me was hard to bury. I needed to sort it all out before I did anything. Like freak the fuck out.

"If Hua Mu Lan has her way, everything in Broken Heart will be toast," said Terran. "Father, I think we should help the Consortium. If Koschei wins, he will"—her gaze slid to me—"make sure the prophecy never comes true."

"If it's a prophecy, doesn't that sorta mean there's no getting around it?" I asked.

"Free will often interferes with the forecasts of seers," said Arin, smiling. "But this prediction seems on course. However, we would be wise not to underestimate Koschei's powers."

"Or Lia's." I wondered what else in Broken Heart had gotten fried thanks to Miss Magnolia Blossom.

Terran planted her butt on the couch next to me. "Koschei can be a very convincing man. Chances are good he's recruited a number of powerful vampires to his side."

Most vampires could bend the wills of humans, but it wasn't the same as having the mind power to control others. Vampires from the Family Koschei could make you think you were in Hawaii when you were really sitting on a glacier.

Arin pulled out a single sheet of paper from a messy stack. He returned to us and sat on the edge of the fountain.

" 'A vampire queen shall come forth from the

place of broken hearts. The seven powers of the Ancients will be hers to command,'" read Arin. "'She shall bind with the outcast, and with this union, she will save the dual-natured. With her consort, she will rule vampires and lycanthropes as one.'"

"None of that says a damned thing about me."

"Astria Vedere's prediction is one in a long line of predictions about the vampires and lycans," said Terran. "They even predicted that you and your friends would be turned into vampires. 'Eleven will Turn; one will burn.'"

Okay, that was scary. Eleven of us single parents had been Turned. I thought about poor Charlene, who'd been Turned with the rest of us. She was the mistress of Jessica's late husband and the mother of Rich, Jr. Rich, Sr., had died because Charlene messed with his car, which led to his fatal accident. She'd burned, all right. She sat on Rich's grave until the sun came up and fried her.

Hysteria welled, but I managed to hang on to my wits. Just because I'd touched two Ancients and might've gotten their powers was no reason to panic. "Unless the oracle gave y'all my name and address, you don't know if I'm the one."

"Yes, we do," said Arin kindly. "You are of the

Family Amahté, the only sect with the power to raise the dead. Rare are Turn-bloods of his line. Aside from Khenti, you are the only Amahté vampire in Broken Heart. Of the ten Turn-bloods left, only you can command spirits and corpses."

"Yuck!" I shivered. "I see ghosts. I don't tell 'em what to do. And I sure as hell have never bossed around a dead body. That's just wrong."

"Ah, yes. Even so, you see that it's only possible for you to command the seven powers," said Arin.

What if I had accumulated the powers of Durga and Lia? Was it the beginning of getting all seven abilities? Foreboding crept through me and my stomach squeezed.

"So I don't guess the Ancients would be real thrilled with a Turn-blood leader?" I asked.

"The lycans would not be happy, either." Gabriel sat on the other side of me. His brows dipped and his lips were pressed together. I knew well that mix of anger and worry. I experienced it all the time as a mother.

"I tire of inaction!" Terran's voice rang with frustration. "I vote we help kick Koschei's ass."

I agreed with her. I didn't want some soulless bastard and his crazy friends marching on my town, trying to kill my family and friends.

"Are you going to introduce me to the others?" I asked. I don't know why I said that. I wasn't sure I could handle any more introductions.

"What others?" asked Terran. "There's only me, my father, Gabriel, and Zerina."

I looked around the perimeter of the room, at those people hanging back in the shadows, watching us all. Ghosts. Damn. It was getting so I couldn't tell the spirits from the humans. I hadn't ever seen so many ghosts in one place.

"Who else is here?" Holding her sword, Terran jumped up from the couch and stalked around the cavern.

"No one who's afraid of your weapons," I admitted wearily. I caught Gabriel's gaze. It was pointed in the direction of my tight T-shirt. I cleared my throat and his head jerked up. Red crawled up his neck to his cheeks.

I nearly laughed. Wasn't that just cute as hell?

"Jeez, Mom!" Wilson threw me a disgusted look. "Can we just leave already? This place sucks."

I didn't want to have it out with him in front of these people. I was getting tired of our fighting and my worrying and his sassing.

"We don't have anywhere to go," I said through clenched teeth, "because our trailer and the beauty shop got blown up. Or did you miss that part while you were seething?"

"You don't care about me!" he screamed, getting to his feet. "I hate you!"

His words hurt, even though I knew, or maybe I hoped, that he didn't truly feel that way. He was hurting all the time, but I was beginning to realize I couldn't fix him. Just like I hadn't been able to fix his father.

"I can put 'im back in the dungeon," offered Zerina.

"Shut up, bitch!" Wilson glared at the fairy, his fists clenched.

Shock roared through me. I'd never heard him speak to a person that way. I raised him better than that! I hadn't figured out how to respond, but Zerina didn't need my help. She didn't even look up from her book. She waved her hand and Wilson flew back onto the couch. She made a closing gesture with her hand and his lips mashed together.

If looks could kill, Wilson would've murdered us all in that instant. He couldn't move or talk, and after a few moments of trying, he gave up.

I couldn't fault Zerina's action. I wished I had that ability. He'd insulted her and brought about his own punishment. A small part of me was glad to see that he was experiencing consequences. God knows I had run out of punishments that worked.

"He gets the point, okay?" I looked at the fairy and realized instantly how to disarm her. "Please, Zerina. Let my son go."

The ire went right out of her. "Oh. Well, if you're going to *beg*."

She waved a hand at him, and my son was freed from her magic. I guess he'd had time to think about his behavior, because he had nothing else to say. He crossed his arms and tried to become one with the couch, his gaze pinned to the floor.

"I sense dark magic," said Zerina.

Gabriel's startled gaze met mine.

My body was jerked upward. For a second, I floated above the couch. Gabriel grabbed at my ankle, but too late. Whatever force held me hostage yanked me backward. I flew across the room.

Terran unsheathed her wicked sword, her gaze sweeping across the cavern. Our enemy was invisible, but not powerless. Her weapon was pulled out of her grip. It tumbled through the air and landed with a splash in the marble fountain.

Gabriel launched over the couch, and Arin pulled out a gun from beneath his robes.

Whatever held me bound my arms, but not my legs. I kicked and screamed as terror scrabbled through me. What was going on? Who was doing this?

My gaze went to Wilson. "Get out of here, Wil!"

"Mom!" he cried. He glared at Gabriel. "Let her go, you asshole!"

"It's not me," said Gabriel. He rammed his shoulder against an invisible wall. Arin tried to approach from the right and Terran from the left. They both met resistance.

"Zerina, take the boy," said Gabriel. "Get him someplace safe."

Mouthy as that fairy was, she didn't argue or hesitate. Zee wrapped her arms around Wilson's shoulders.

My son's terrified gaze never left mine as he and his rescuer disappeared in a pink flash. Relief skittered through my fear. At least my son was safe.

"Patricia!" Gabriel shouted, his fists striking the unseen barrier. "Patricia!"

I kicked for all I was worth and screamed myself hoarse. It was like being encased in brick. I couldn't free myself. I wasn't Zenlike in the best of moments. Panic and terror were making mincemeat of my sanity.

Patrick and Zerina popped into the cave behind Gabriel, gold sparkles dissipating. Patrick held a pair of short swords.

"Zee?" asked Terran, her shocked gaze taking in Patrick.

"He followed me," groused Zerina. "He's Sidhe, too."

"My, my . . . aren't you popular?" growled a voice next to my ear. The gray-skinned demon appeared; his massive arms tight around my waist. Shit-oh-shit-oh-shit.

"Andhaka," I whispered.

The demon hissed. He loosed one of his arms and said words in a language I didn't understand. A silver dagger materialized in his hand. He pressed the sharp blade against my throat.

Fear cha-chaed through me. Dread settled like a cold, hard lump in my stomach.

"Please. Don't." I hated the pitiful sound of my own words.

His arm tightened around my waist.

"You can't harm her with that," said Patrick, "much less remove her head."

Gee, thanks, Patrick. Give the demon ideas, why don't you. I glared at him, but his eyes were on Andhaka.

"I can hurt her plenty if the blade is poisoned with demon blood." He pulled the knife away long enough to drag it along the arm clutching my stomach. When he returned it to my throat, the sulfur stink of his black blood made me gag.

Patrick blanched. Zee's gaze went wide.

Gabriel smashed the barrier with his fist. "Don't hurt her, you demon bastard!"

"What's your bargain?" asked Arin.

"No!" cried Patrick.

"Desperate times call for desperate measures," said Arin. "What do you want, Andhaka?"

"Many things," said the demon. "You are all fools. You expect the *loup de sang* to live peacefully among vampires and lycans?"

"When Patricia is queen, he will be her consort," challenged Arin.

"Queen?" Patrick's eyes bulged. "You think Patsy is the one who will rule vampires and lycans as one people? *Are you crazy?*"

I took offense at Patrick's incredulous tone, even though I had no intention of being a queen of anyfuckingthing. Hmph. I'd never felt so underestimated and undervalued in all my life. Just because I knew how to add highlights and do a killer pageboy cut didn't mean I was a dumb-ass. I could rule if I wanted to, thank you very much.

Patrick must've seen my expression because he sobered up right quick. "Patsy, I didn't mean—"

"Hel-*lo*! Hostage of a demon here."

"What's the bargain?" asked Arin again, his voice edged with desperation. "What will you take in exchange for the life of Patricia?"

"I must follow the wishes of my mistress," said Andhaka.

"She is not here," said Arin slyly. "She won't know about our deal."

"I beg to differ." Durga appeared in the blink of an eye. She looked like a representative of the Lollipop Guild standing next to the huge demon. Yet it was obvious she held all the power. From the position of her hands, I knew she was the one creating the shield that kept the others away.

"Enough of this stalling," she said. "Andhaka, slit her throat!"

Durga

Translated from the Memoirs of Ruadan

Durga was a high priestess for an ancient cult that used demons in their rituals.

She was in her late forties, considered long-lived nearly four millennia ago. She reminded me of a small, dark bird. She was tiny, her eyes never missing a single detail, her movements concise and graceful. Yet she possessed an awesome and dark power: calling forth and dispelling demons.

In modern times, Durga's people were called the Indus Valley Civilization or the Harappan Civilization.

I discovered her in a smoking ruin, wounded

and dying. The abilities of the priestesses had been so feared by outsiders, they had been attacked and their temple destroyed.

Durga was the only survivor.

As with Koschei and Lia, I knew that Durga was special. Her unique abilities would be useful to our kind, and so, I offered her immortality and a place on the Council.

The Turning was especially difficult and I feared she might not make it. But survive it she did. I would learn not to underestimate this woman. Anyone who assumed she was weak, did so at their own peril.

She was eager to leave the valley, and asked to continue with me. I was glad of the company, especially since our journey took us through what is now Pakistan and Afghanistan and through, Iran, Iraq, and Israel.

When we reached Saudi Arabia, we took a boat across the channel into the land of the Nubians, in what is known today as the Sudan.

Chapter 13

The knife pressed against my throat. The demon's poison burned my flesh.

"Stop!" I screamed. "Stop it *now*!"

To my utter shock, he removed the knife.

"What are you doing?" Durga snapped. "How dare you listen to a Turn-blood over your own mistress!"

"I . . . must . . . obey . . . her," the demon managed between clenched teeth. "She . . . has . . . your . . . magic."

Whoa. Wait. Her magic? Oh my God. I had gotten her power.

Wide-eyed, Durga stared at me. I wasn't

gonna give her the opportunity to do me in. Of course, she was a little busy holding off my would-be rescuers.

"Let me go, Andhaka," I demanded.

He dropped me like a stone. Ji-*mo*-ney! It was working!

"Give me the knife."

He handed the silver dagger to me, his eyes filled with hatred.

"Stop obeying that Turn-blood," Durga screeched.

Power pulsed through me. It was as though an electrical switch had been flipped. I felt as if I were outside of my own body, observing a more powerful, ancient vampire.

I pressed the knife against Durga's throat. "How do you like it?"

"Mistress!"

I pointed at Andhaka without looking at him. "Go to hell. Never return."

Durga's skin started to burn, but her eyes showed no fear. She was too much of an Ancient to reveal such a human emotion. "You've banished my favorite slave," she said softly. "For that, you will pay."

She jerked away from me. Before I could stop her, she sparkled away. Damn Ancients and their disappearing acts.

Gabriel reached me first. He yanked the knife out of my hand and tossed it away. He held me tightly, pressing kisses into my hair.

For a long moment, no one said anything.

Patrick was the first to break the eerie silence. "We should all get to the compound."

Gabriel and I parted, holding hands as we turned to face the others.

"Even us outlaws?" asked Arin.

Patrick nodded.

"It's safer for us here," said Arin. "Prophecy or not, most vampires and lycans do not welcome us."

"Patsy?"

I knew what Patrick was asking. It was time for me to go to the compound. My son was there. As much as Zerina hated those who ran this town and who ruled the vampires, she'd done the best thing for Wilson. I owed her.

"Patricia." Gabriel imbued my name with anguish, with regret. I felt an answering pain in my own heart, but I quelled it. I wouldn't fall into this trap again. He needed me? Well, I didn't need him. I didn't need anyone. I'd learned the hard way how to stand on my own two feet.

Gabriel released my hand and I moved away from him. Anguish shimmered in his eyes. My life had been ripped apart all over again, but this time there was no rebuilding it from the ashes.

"Please," he murmured. "Please."

Y'know, for a second there I almost caved. I actually entertained the idea of throwing myself into Gabriel's arms and telling Patrick to take a flying leap. See, that's what is so bad about lust. It makes you do stupid things.

"I can't stay here, Gabriel. I can't accept . . . that I'm part of some prophecy. That I'm destined to be with you. I run my own life." Because I was a coward, I whirled around and walked to Patrick.

He sheathed his swords. I accepted his embrace and put my head against his shoulder, refusing to look back. He wrapped his arms around me.

Having your atoms dissembled and rearranged was a strange sensation. Y'know how when your leg falls asleep and you get that heavy prickling sensation? It's like that, only a thousand times worse.

The minute we arrived wherever it was, I nearly fell over. We were in the main section of the new Broken Heart library, which was located in the compound. My first impression was endless shelves filled with lots of books. We were near a long wooden table obviously used for studying. Chairs were scattered around it randomly and books lay in careless stacks across its surface.

"Where's my son?" I croaked.

"Mom!" He bolted down the aisle and I opened my arms to him. Wilson grabbed me and held me tightly. My shirt got wet with his tears, and man alive, I wanted to cry, too. Instead, I let Wilson weep for the both of us.

"I'm glad you're okay," he said. "I thought he was going to kill you."

"I'm okay," I said. "I'll never abandon you, Wil. Never."

He nodded. "I know, Mom."

"Wil, honey," said Jessica gently, "we need to talk to your mom."

Wilson stopped hugging me, but as he turned around to face Jess, he shook his head. "No. I'm not leaving."

"Just for a little while," she said. "I'll take you to where the other kids are staying. Tamara's there."

The mention of Tamara got Wilson's interest. He had a sorta crush on her, even though she had a vampire-hunting boyfriend named Durriken. He only popped into town every now and again, though.

"Mom?"

I nodded to him. "You go on now. I'll see you soon."

He kissed my cheek, his eyes filled with apologies I knew he couldn't say. It was okay, though. We'd hit a turning point in our relationship. I guess I could thank Gabriel for that blessing.

I looked at the others who waited around the table. Jessica had taken Wilson to the other kids, which left Patrick and Ruadan. His expression was grim. He pointed to a chair. "We need to talk."

"Yeah, that's exactly what I want to do." I dropped into the chair. "I take it that Koschei's causing hell again."

Patrick nodded. "You were right, Patsy. We set a trap. We let it be known the next Council meeting would be held here. We tried to get everyone into the compound." He looked at me with brows raised. I shrugged. "And we bulked up our security. We believed we had prepared for the worst."

"Apparently not," offered Lorcan as he joined us at the long table. His wife, Eva, was with him. She smiled at me and waved. I was glad to see her. She was nice to talk to, even though she liked to use ten-dollar words. Jessica rounded the bookshelf and took her place next to Patrick.

"Lia and Durga decided to go to the dark side," I said. "You didn't count on that."

"No," admitted Ruadan. "We didn't count on a lot of things."

"Do they have the Taint?" I asked.

Patrick looked confused and Lorcan horrified. He shared a look with his wife, then asked, "The Taint?"

"No," said Ruadan. "Impossible."

"Does it matter?" I pressed. "We have the cure, right?"

At one of the many meetings the Consortium liked to convene, they had announced that a cure was imminent, thanks to Lorcan using himself as a guinea pig. Then they'd never released it or said another word about it. Probably because of the shape-shifting side effects. But I wanted to hear the truth from my friends.

"Royal lycan blood from live donors kills the Taint," I said. Huh. I guess I had paid attention to Dr. Michaels' dry and uninteresting lecture.

"That's what we said, yes." Lorcan grimaced. He glanced at his father and Ruadan nodded sharply.

"Based on our results with Faustus, we believed we had the cure within our grasp. We've been trying to synthetically replicate the original blood donations, but we haven't been able to do so."

"Whatever cure you cooked up relies on the real blood," I surmised. Hey, not bad for a blonde, right? "And that means there's no way to make enough antidotes for all the Tainted vampires—at least not quickly."

Lorcan nodded. Ever since he and Eva hooked up, he'd ditched the all-black look and was more prone to smiling. Not that I spent all that much time with them. They liked books and getting into debates about word origins, which I found boring as hell.

"But there is also a side effect. A big one," he said. "It's why no one after Faustus was given the cure."

I already knew this part, thanks to Gabriel. Anger pulsed through me. I'd been lied to by these people. It made no never mind to me if hybrids existed. If Gabriel had been ostracized because he shared their condition, I understood his rage.

Lorcan stepped away from the table and into the aisle. Before my astonished gaze, his body started to change. His clothes ripped and fell away in tatters as his human form crumpled and elongated and sprouted fur. After a few minutes, I was staring at his new shape.

He was a lycanthrope.

I stared at him. "Yeah, that's a side effect, all right."

Lorcan barked his agreement, then padded down the aisle out of sight. My gaze went to Eva. She'd had the Taint, too, and been cured. She nodded. "I can do it, too. The ability manifests within two months of the blood transfusion."

"You can see why we're reluctant to give the cure to every Tainted vampire," said Lorcan as he rounded the tall bookshelf and smiled. I was relieved to see him clothed again.

"There's a big difference when the blood is taken from live, royal lycans," said Ruadan. "Dead blood from any lycan caused the mutations."

After the first crazy—and now dead—leader of the Wraiths had experimented on Tainted vampires, he'd created a creature caught between vampire and lycanthrope—a big, hairy monster that walked on two legs and still had the vampire disease.

"Well, if Lor and Eva can do it and nobody's trying to kill them," I said, "then why is Gabriel running for his life?" My gaze shifted to Patrick. "Why can't we offer him and his friends protection?"

"Those are excellent questions," said Eva. Her gaze bounced between the men. Lorcan flinched. Apparently, his wife had already brought up this concern. "Gabriel was born a lycan-vampire. He has the capabilities of lycan-thropes and vampires, without the physiological repercussions."

"You mean they're not undead, but can still do what we can do?"

She nodded. "I've been researching it for months. Once I started shifting, I wanted to know everything I could."

"A *stóirín*," said Lorcan in a low voice. "We've already discussed this issue."

"No, I've talked about it and you stubbornly refuse to consider that I'm right." Eva glowered at him. I saw Eva's gaze on me. "What was Gabriel like?"

That was a loaded question I couldn't begin to answer. Handsome. Sexy. Murderous.

"I think the *loup de sang* may be the solution to the lycanthrope's fertility problems," she said.

"Eva—"

"No!" She moved away from her husband and walked to where I was sitting on the edge of the table. "Patsy's in this up to her neck. She deserves to know."

From the pile on the table, she chose a large,

thick book and opened it. When she found the section she wanted, she pointed to the top of the elaborately decorated page.

Hell, I mostly read magazines, not having the patience or the attention span for a whole novel. This piece of literature seemed important (and short), so I leaned over and read it.

Chapter 14

Legend of the Moon Goddess and Her Sons

Long ago when men still believed in magic and honored its Makers, the Goddess of the Moon often visited Earth. Of all Earth's creatures, she loved wolves the best, and to them she gave her blessings and protections.

The Goddess wanted children, so she took her wolf form and mated with an alpha named Tark. He was a fierce warrior, a loyal protector, and a skilled hunter.

These were the qualities she wanted for her sons.

Under the full moon, she gave birth to twins. The firstborn was a wolf of black. And the second, a wolf of gray.

Her older son had the ability to turn from human to wolf. However, her second born could assume his wolf nature only on the night of the full moon.

The Black Wolf became a warrior even greater than his own father. He became a loyal protector of his kind; his battle prowess was legendary.

The Gray Wolf became a hunter so skilled that he could use any manner of weapon and he could track any of Earth's animals. He learned to hide his true nature so that he could live among humans.

The Moon Goddess' sons grew lonely. They wanted wives and families. The Goddess offered her firstborn a beautiful female wolf, which she gave the ability to shift into human.

To her second born, the Goddess gave a beautiful female human. Since her son assumed his wolf form only during the full moon, she gave his mate the same ability.

This is the story told from father to son,

mother to daughter, of the lycanthrope heritage. Some are full-bloods, shifting whenever they need, and others, the Roma, shifting only on the full moon.

"The full-bloods are dying out, Patsy," said Eva. "Damian did something no full-blood had done before—he mated with a Roma. Their children were the hope that Black Wolf's line wouldn't die. But after his wife was killed, he discovered that the babies were mutated. He forbade any more unions between full-bloods and the Roma."

It took me a while to assimilate all this information. I still felt like shit and now, I also felt horribly sad. I began to understand why Damian and other lycans loathed Gabriel. He represented their greatest fears. He wasn't lycan or vampire, but both. Eva was right. Gabriel might very well be the answer to their infertility problems.

My world started to spin. Closing my eyes made it worse, so I opened them again and pressed a hand against my roiling stomach.

"Does a wolfie marriage work like a vampire's?" I asked. "You know, is there a time limit? And if one dies, does the other one share the same fate?"

"Most lycans mate for life. If their spouse dies, they will not. Some mate again. Others live out the remainder of their lives alone," she said. "But one thing remains the same—the full-bloods aren't reproducing. Even if a female lycan becomes pregnant, she will be lucky if she has two babies. And of those, she will be lucky if even one lives to its first year. Damian believed that all hope for the werewolves was lost ... which is why he courted a Roma bride."

"The prophecy says something about the dual-natured," I said. "This new ruler is supposed to save the wolfies? Maybe Gabriel is part of the prophecy."

"Except that he's not," interrupted Ruadan. "The oracle remained vague about how she will help the lycans, but it certainly gives our guardians reason to help the prophecy along."

Jessica returned. The others started talking amongst themselves and I zoned out. This was the longest night ever.

"Enough," said Ruadan, ending whatever debate was raging.

"Dad ..." This entreaty came from Patrick. "There are ten Broken Heart Turn-bloods."

"Nine, since the oracle pinpointed a female."

Patrick's gaze flicked to me. "Arin said that Patsy was the foretold ruler."

"What?" Ruadan studied me, frowning. He looked as disbelieving as his son had earlier. Well, wasn't that a pip? Patrick had thrown me to the wolves, so to speak, to wrest his wife out of their teeth. Nice.

"Not that I'm interested in being your leader, but it'd be nice if you wouldn't act that surprised at the possibility."

Patrick looked at Jessica. I'd been told that bound vampires could speak to each other telepathically. Jessica told me once that Patrick and Lorcan could talk to each other that way, too.

"She can do the fire thing," said Jessica.

"And the demon thing," added Patrick. "Andhaka released her just because she demanded it."

Ruadan stared at me, his silver eyes filled with secrets. "Is it true you can wield fire?"

He put his hand on my shoulder and I lifted mine to cover his. The moment my skin touched his, a jolt of electric heat rolled right through me. The power of the surge nearly knocked me out of the chair.

Strangely, Ruadan didn't seem to notice.

The silence was thick. I looked around at them all and saw the shock and concern in each of their faces.

"I just did it one time," I said, feeling defensive.

"Try again," Ruadan said.

"No!" Lorcan and Eva shouted together. They looked sheepish, but Eva gestured at the bookshelves. "It's too flammable in here."

"I'll make sure the fire is extinguished," said a new voice. The man was dressed in Armani. The brown pinstripe enhanced his olive skin and amber eyes. He had the tall, lean build of a runner. He wore his curly brown hair short, which complemented his classic Italian looks. A platinum Rolex gleamed from his left wrist. The gold ring on his right pinky featured a two-carat, square-cut diamond. In one hand he held a large glass.

He twitched his fingers over it and two strands of water emerged. He created a square, a circle, and a triangle. Then the water splashed back into its cup.

"So your Family power is making water dance?" I asked.

"His name is Velthur," said Ruadan. "He's one of the seven Ancients."

Velthur grinned. "I can do a lot more, Patsy. If it's liquid, then I can control it."

"So, show us your skills," said Jessica.

I really didn't want to try starting a fire or

calling a demon. I wished I could do the flash-outta-here thing or even fly. I closed my eyes, trying to gain some perspective. Yeah, wouldn't it be great if I could just float away?

"Um . . . Patsy?"

Jessica's voice sounded farther away. I opened my eyes and found myself looking down at my friends. I *was* floating and I was close to the ceiling. "Hey! How do I get down?"

"You think about it," called up Ruadan.

I was too panicked to think about anything but falling. So, that's what I did. I screamed and flailed my arms. Luckily for me, Ruadan was faster, and he managed to grab hold of me before I splattered all over the library floor.

I returned to my chair and held on to the armrests. Maybe flying wasn't such a great Family power.

"How did you do that?" asked Ruadan.

"You must've transferred your power when you touched me or I touched you."

"You touched Lia and Durga, too?"

I nodded. "I felt this . . . electrical surge."

"She has four Family powers," said Velthur. He walked to me, leaned down, and gripped my shoulder. Zip-zap. Heat raced through me and once again, I felt as if I'd been electrified.

Velthur stepped back and held out the cup of water. "Go on," he said.

"Go on and what?"

"Make the water dance."

If thought was the key to controlling the powers of the Ancients, then I should be able to think about the water taking shape, and it would. I looked at the cup and imagined the water inside rising up and forming a heart.

The liquid wiggled up like a clear snake, then swooped into the heart. It shimmered there, until I released it. The water splashed back into the cup.

"Holy shit," said Jessica. She looked as shocked as I felt. "Patsy's the freaking queen."

"Whoopee," I said.

"Atta girl." Ruadan patted me on the shoulder.

"We should get to the shelter," said Lorcan. "It'll be dawn soon."

"If you don't mind, I'll stay here a few minutes," I said. I was having a hard time wrapping my brain around the truth. I was the new ruler. And if I was the queen of the Vedere prophecy, then the outlaw was surely Gabriel.

"That's either faith or bullshit," I muttered.

"The compound is shielded by Wiccan spells," said Patrick, "but we don't know how long they'll last against an extended attack. There are only three entrances into the shelter."

I switched my attention to Patrick. Yeah. Why give an enemy too many opportunities to breach security?

"Across the courtyard are the Consortium's headquarters. Get to the basement. Go to the far back wall. You'll see what to do next."

"Okay dokay."

Everyone told me good-bye, and I was glad to be alone. I really did want some time to think and figure out what to do next. With my home and business gone, it was probably time to admit I needed to move into the compound. As much as I hated what it represented, it would be the safest place for my son.

Wait a minute. What was I thinking? The leaders of the vampires and lycans weren't gonna just let me waltz in and take over. Maybe Broken Heart wasn't any safer for me and Wil than it was for Gabriel. Jeez! Wasn't there an instruction manual or something?

"Patricia."

Shocked, I looked up into the gold gaze of Gabriel. It was as if by thinking about him, I had conjured him.

"What are you doing here?"

"I wanted to see you." He walked to me and

knelt by my chair, his hands resting on my thighs. "The compound is not without its weaknesses." His fingers stroked my jeans. "Are you all right?"

"Dandy." The urge to control myself didn't last long. I rose from my chair, shoving him over. He fell on his ass, staring up at me. Then he jumped to his feet.

His gold eyes flashed with anger and he growled. I went lust-hot at that low rumble. Oowee! I wanted to jump his bones. Just rip off his clothes and lick him. He saw that need in me, too.

"I'm just me, Patsy the hair dresser." I wanted to believe it, I really did.

I stalked toward Gabriel with every intention of walloping him. Why had he followed me here? I was furious with him. With myself. Mostly, I was pissed off because I wanted to be wanted for me. Just for me. Not for what I could do or what I represented. Admitting that to myself was hard. Sometimes, the truth hurt. A lot.

I got close enough to poke him in the chest. Gabriel leaned forward and I swore he was sniffing me. "You are glorious when you're mad," he whispered. He grabbed my wrists and pulled me snug against him. "I want you," he said in a low voice. "I can't stop thinking about you. You're in my head, in my heart."

His words weren't slick or charming. They were raw, real. If I'd had a working heart, it would've been trying to hammer out of my chest.

"Gabriel . . ."

He kissed me. More like his lips conquered mine. I wrested my hands out of his grip and wrapped my arms around his neck. His tongue thrust inside my mouth, and electric lust zapped me.

God, the man made me hot.

He pulled away, his gaze dark with desire. "Admit that you're mine."

Chapter 15

Gabriel kissed me roughly. "Never leave me again. Especially not with that pretty boy Patrick."

I laughed. "Pretty boy Patrick is very married. And he's got nothing on you, honey."

All the same, doubt seeped through the primal beat of my passion. I couldn't shake the idea that Gabriel was only chasing me because he thought I was going to have power. I couldn't fault the man for seeking protection for himself or his friends. Still, I didn't want to be used. Not by anyone for any reason.

"It'll be dawn soon," I said. "I need to get to the shelter."

Gabriel caressed my cheek. "Wilson's safer there . . . and you want to be with him."

"Yeah."

"C'mon then."

We walked down the main path that led to the Consortium headquarters. The compound was mostly empty. No one had said boo to us, and I could only imagine it was because everyone was in the shelter. I was anxious to get to Wilson. I wanted him to know I was okay. I didn't want things to reverse between us.

I hadn't seen Darrius, Drake, or Damian in a while. My guess was that they were guarding the Ancients. Nobody was a better guardian than those three. I glanced at Gabriel and smiled. Well, maybe one.

The roses and other sweet flowers perfumed the courtyard. Had it been any other night, I might've enjoyed holding Gabriel's hand as we hurried along the path.

About halfway across, I heard a terrible scream. It sounded like a cross between a lion's roar and a bird's squawking. I looked up and saw the damnedest thing I'd ever seen.

A dragon.

I stopped, which was a stupid thing to do. I

just couldn't believe my eyes. The scales were yellow with red stripes and the wings were huge. The eyes were black as night and the snout crusted with soot. Its monster feet had some seriously sharp talons.

It hovered above the courtyard and every time it tried to go down, it bounced upward—as if it were hitting a trampoline. The Wiccan protection spells were doing their work. I'd have to offer those ladies and gents some free haircuts.

The dragon let out another frustrated shriek. As it turned to its side to circle and try again, I saw the rider on its back.

Ol' Magnolia Blossom.

She raised her arm and a fireball erupted from her palm. The fiery orb looked as if it would hit me spot-on, but the second it hit the "bubble," it went out like a match doused in water.

I didn't need another hint. Gabriel tugged on my hand and we jaunted across the courtyard in record time. We scrambled down to the basement.

I hurried to the far back wall. There wasn't a sign, much less a door. A shiny, very sharp gold nail stuck out of the concrete wall about eye level. I peered at it and snorted. "And what am I supposed to do with that?"

"It's a blood lock," he said. "You have to

pierce your finger with it." He nodded toward the lock. "Only those whose blood was included in the enchantment will open the door."

I didn't recall a time when I gave my blood to the Consortium for a spell. Not that they would've asked, much less told me about all this mess. I was skeptical about it working, but I raised my hand to try.

Boom! The whole building shook. The force of the impact pushed me off the wall, and the two of us staggered away, trying to regain our balance.

Boom! The ceiling cracked. Pieces started dropping from the ceiling like gray snow.

"What the hell are they using to get in?" I asked. "A nuclear bomb?"

"They've breached the barrier. Lia knows we're somewhere in the building." Gabriel took my hand and pulled me toward the blood lock. "You need to get inside."

I pushed my forefinger onto the nail. Blood dripped onto it.

Nothing happened.

"Shit, shit, shit!" I rubbed my bloodied finger along the top and underside of the nail.

No door appeared.

We heard an ominous crack. Then the roar-squawk of the dragon echoed far above us. Had they destroyed the headquarters? Was that beast tromping around the debris, trying to sniff us out or whatever it was that dragons did to find people?

I tried poking another finger, and when that didn't work, I plunged my wrist against the sharp point. No matter which location it came from, my blood was not opening the god-damned door.

I looked at Gabriel, panicked. "You try it."

The dragon's cry was much closer. Of all the ways I thought my end would come, I had never believed it would be by dragon. A bottle of tequila and a dare gone wrong, sure. But being fried by a crazy vampire's pet? Nope.

"It won't work for me." He drew my hands into his. The wounds had healed, but there was still blood on me. Gabriel didn't seem to notice. He kissed each of my wrists. "We must return to the cave."

"But my son is in there!" I cried.

"There are at least a hundred vampires in that shelter, not to mention a dozen guardians. He's far safer there than anywhere else."

We were running out of choices. Either we made a break for it in the next few minutes, or we ended up prisoners—or worse, the kind of dead that was permanent.

We stood there for nearly a minute while the ominous sounds above us got louder. Koschei and his minions were surely all over the place by now.

"Oh! I have my cell phone! I'll call someone and they'll let us in from the other side." Excited about this option, I broke free of his embrace and dug the phone out from my front pocket.

The battery was dead.

More noises sounded above us, but they were farther away now. They hadn't yet found the entrance to the basement.

I had to grapple with the idea of a partner who carried his share of the burden. It was more than that, actually. Gabriel wasn't arguing with me or trying to make me feel bad or telling me he wasn't responsible for what my friends did. He was helping me. He was shouldering my duty because . . . well, I didn't know, did I? I couldn't quite comprehend a man who simply took my word, who quieted my worry, who stood at my side.

I wanted to cry. Or to yell "yippee!" It was a toss-up, but I was leaning toward "yippee!"

"We have to sneak outta here." I looked at Gabriel. He was concentrating on the stairs, his shimmering hair drifting carelessly over his shoulders. He was so beautiful.

"Don't you have a phone?" I asked.

He grimaced. "I lost it in the woods. When I saw what was happening to you and Khenti, I went wolf as fast as I could."

I was feeling those warm fuzzies again. I'm not exactly a low maintenance, quiet, sweet-natured kind of girl. That independence and sass were hard won, let me tell you, and I had no plans to give up who I was, flaws and all. But Gabriel made me want to be a better person.

The noises above us had faded into silence. We crept toward the stairs. For all my hooting and hollering about testosterone-fueled decisions, I didn't complain when Gabriel tucked me behind as he peered up the staircase.

All we saw was darkness. Earlier the lights had been on, so either they'd gotten knocked out or they'd been turned off.

Gabriel went up the stairs slowly and I followed. We tried to be as quiet as possible, but my boots didn't have a soft tread and my occasional clicks on the concrete made us both flinch.

When we reached the top, we could see that the door had fallen off, mostly because the entrance had cracked and released the framing. Even though it looked like the building had sustained serious damage, it was still intact.

Patsy. The voice whispered inside my head. *Come to me, Patsy. That's right. This way.*

I felt the most insane need to follow the man's directions. He had such a beautiful voice. Gabriel's hand tugged on mine, but I shook free of his grip. As if in a dream, I walked down the hallway.

The man was down there. He wanted me. And I needed him. He would give me . . . I blinked. Give me what?

Anything you desire.

I felt Gabriel's hand catch my arm and he dragged me backward. I stumbled. My feet didn't want to go back. They wanted to go forward. To him.

Gabriel latched on to my shoulders and held me still. I reared back my head and slammed it into his. His hands slid off my shoulders as he collapsed to the floor. I looked down and saw him unconscious.

Good girl, said the voice. *He doesn't love you, Patsy. He doesn't really want you. He wants what you can give him. He's just like Sean.*

A tall, slim man emerged from the darkness. His eyes were a shade too light of brown and his shaggy brown hair was drawn into a ponytail.

He wore white from head to toe—a short-sleeved shirt, white dress pants, and shiny white shoes. His face was long and gaunt, his chin pointy. Two gold hoops sparkled from each ear. His thin lips were pulled into a coaxing smile.

"So you're the big threat?" he asked, amused. His Russian accent was slight. "To me, you look like a woman easily controlled."

"Yes," I agreed. "I'm whatever you say I am."

"Of course you are." He patted my cheek. "I'm afraid that you and your mongrel boyfriend must die."

Zela

Translated from the Memoirs of Ruadan

Zela's statuesque beauty and graceful nature bespoke her life as a Nubian princess. Her smooth skin was like dark chocolate. Her hair was cropped short. However, her loveliness could not protect her from her father's greed.

She had the unique ability to manipulate metals of all kinds. Her father had confined her, refusing to allow her to marry or have children, so that she could make weapons for their tribe. The night she attempted suicide, I found her and Turned her.

I should say that Durga found her. She had been using her favorite demon, Andhaka, to scout for us. He was very good at finding routes around towns, shelters that protected us during our days, and guarding us while we slept.

I don't know why Andhaka reported to us about the beautiful girl who had stabbed herself with a silver dagger. As a demon, he held no regard for human despair, much less human lives. His interest was the sword. He wanted his mistress to gift it to him.

I wanted to see the girl.

We glamoured those guarding her rooms and entered. Zela's stomach was a mess and her blood pooled darkly on the clean-swept floor.

Durga saw to her wound, but Zela's mortal life was draining away.

Again, it was Andhaka who told us about Zela's ability. He'd watched her create the dagger from chunks of silver that she had melted and molded with her magic.

As she breathed her last, I offered Zela immortality.

She could not answer. I could not interpret the look in her eyes. I didn't know what to do. But Durga did.

"Turn her," she said softly. "She has much to offer the world. If she wants freedom, you can give her that and more."

We stole her from the palace and took her to our cave. I performed the Turning ritual.

When we awoke the next evening, we knew Zela had survived the process. She told us that the gods surely had plans for her; that we must've been sent to save her.

I wanted to go to Egypt, but Durga and Zela wanted to strike out for other lands. They decided to travel together. I knew they would be safe, especially with Andhaka protecting them. Because he had saved Zela, she gave him the dagger that took her life.

The next evening, I made a pact with Zela and Durga. They, too, would serve on the Council and agreed to show up at the meeting place.

I wished them well and headed north.

Chapter 16

"Die?" Faint fear pulsed through me.

"*Ssshhh*," said the man. "Your sacrifice will still usher in the new age of parakind. I like to think of it as the age of Koschei."

His hands took mine, and the moment our skin connected, twin bolts of electric heat zapped me. My head snapped up as the fog in my mind cleared instantly.

"You will calm yourself, Patsy. You will—"

I thought about Lia's fire. I imagined the flames dancing from my palms to Koschei's smug face.

Flames burst from my hands and shot toward

him. He moved out of the way so fast, I couldn't track him, not even with my vampire vision.

"It seems I've underestimated you," he said, chuckling. "I will not do so again."

He disappeared in a flash of gold sparks. Jeez. Did everyone know how to do that, or what?

I whirled around and hurried to Gabriel. He'd regained consciousness and was sitting up, rubbing his forehead.

"Oh my God! I'm so sorry. Are you okay, baby?"

"I'll live," he said. "But you have to promise to kiss my boo-boos later."

We stood up, and I launched myself into Gabriel's arms. I was so upset that I'd nearly been glamoured into danger that I was dry-crying. God, I missed a good old-fashioned wail.

Gabriel kissed the top of my head. "It's okay, sweetheart. You're stronger than he is."

I needed to hear those very words. How did he know just what to say, just what to do? His arms tightened around me. That emotion I refused to name welled within me. But I couldn't say it. Not yet.

No one was in the cavern. As I followed Gabriel through the empty room, I looked at the marble fountain. It was such an odd thing to have in a cave. But it was obviously an important symbol to Gabriel and his pack. I still couldn't place the woman, but the wolf reminded me of Gabriel.

We entered a narrow hallway dimly lit by small, white orbs. A few feet down, I heard the sounds of water. Gabriel made a left, and when I entered the small cave, I saw that a few fairy lights danced in here, as well. The waterfall sprayed down from the top of the craggy wall and into a shallow basin.

"What's this?"

"A waterfall," he said. "I thought we could get naked under it."

My nonexistent heart skipped a beat. Lust beat low and hot in my belly, but I wasn't ready to just jump on the marriage train.

Gabriel had no such doubts.

He undressed and I feasted on his nakedness. I licked my lips, my body going white-hot. He stepped under the water and I watched, the happy voyeur, as he ran his hands over himself. His fingers roved down his muscled chest and over his thighs. His long, white hair dripped like silver down his taut backside.

"Patricia?"

I heard the question he infused in my name. His golden gaze snared mine, and for a moment,

I couldn't speak. I wanted more than anything to get out of my clothes and step into that water with him. I wanted to touch him and I wanted to be touched. But I couldn't still the doubts or the questions.

"You're the outlaw," I said. I watched water squiggle down his pectorals. "The one mentioned in the prophecy."

"Yes."

"It appears I'm doomed to bind with you."

"Doomed?" He chuckled. "You need me, Patricia. Only if we bind can we hope to defeat Koschei. He's trying to make sure the prophecy does not come true, but he's too late."

"You saved me," I said. "I owe you."

He shook his head. "I don't want you to bind with me because of a debt."

"I'm willing, isn't that enough?"

For a moment, only the soft splash of the waterfall infiltrated the silence. Jeez! This meeting my destiny head-on stuff wasn't so easy.

Gabriel stepped out of the water, looped his fingers around my wrists, and pulled me against him. My clothes got soaked, but I hardly cared.

"You are so stubborn. You guard your heart, even though you know it already belongs to me." A growl vibrated in his words. "You drive me wild, Patricia."

I didn't know if he was angry or turned on or both. His eyes narrowed. Yeah. Both. He let go of my hands and cupped my ass, pressing me intimately against his hard-on.

His kiss was possessive. He thrust his tongue into my mouth and I responded. How could I not? My nipples hardened, pressing against his muscled chest. I wrapped my arms around his neck and melted against him.

He pulled back, his mouth swollen and his eyes shiny with lust. "Do you want me?"

"More than my next pint."

He looked indecisive, and then he sighed. "What if I told you that I could break our binding?"

"That's impossible." Oddly enough I was disappointed in his offer of a get-out-of-binding-free card. I had feelings for him, but I refused to even think the L-word. Lord knows I wanted to jump his bones something awful. I knew it was right, binding with him. Sometimes, you took a leap of faith—and hoped you didn't fall off the cliff.

"Just so we're clear," I said, "I'm the queen of vampires and lycans. You're the outlaw and my consort. We're going to bind, have steamy-hot sex, and tomorrow, we'll kick Koschei and company's ass."

He nodded. Then he stepped out of the water-fall and helped me out of my clothes.

Maybe I was the queen destined to rule the vampires. But at this moment, I felt like Gabriel's queen. Beloved. Honored. Worshipped.

We stood together under the spray of cold water. We washed each other slowly, with no soap or loofahs, only our hands. We did a thorough job, too, from head to toe. I wished I'd had shampoo to lather into his lovely hair, but I figured I'd get a chance another time.

"I claim you." Gabriel put his hand on my neck and said, "You are mine."

Heat flashed. I put my hand on Gabriel's neck and said, "You are mine."

"I give you my words." He drew away from me slightly and stared into my eyes. "I will serve you faithfully, Patricia. I gladly bind with you. I gladly give you my heart."

His word giving made my nonexistent pulse jump. "I will honor you for all of my days, Gabriel. I'm the happiest I've ever been with you."

Something electric arced between us. The magic of the binding wound around us.

"Now, it's time to mate," he said roughly.

It didn't take long for gentle caresses to give way to more sensual exploration. His skin was smooth as silk and felt so wonderful under my hands and my lips. Not even the cold water could keep me from getting hot.

He palmed my nipples; then he twisted them between nimble fingers. Pleasure shot down to the point between my thighs and I moaned.

I reached down and rubbed his velvety cock. It was big and hard and oh-so-yummy. My actions were rewarded by a deep growl and a nip on my shoulder. Oo-wee!

Gabriel's eyes captured mine.

"You are mine," he said, his voice rumbling.

"And vice versa," I said, grinning.

He backed me against the wall and pushed his cock into the wet vee of my thighs. "Do you want me?"

"Only more than anything," I whispered.

His hands slid under my buttocks and he lifted me, as if I were a feather. That was a sexy move, sure enough.

Then he impaled me with one swift stroke of his cock.

Oh, Lord.

I wrapped my legs around his waist and clutched his shoulders, my gaze held hostage by his. He thrust inside me, growling deep in his throat, as he took his pleasure, as he gave me pleasure.

He made me shudder all the way to my pedicured toes.

His eyes glittered like yellow diamonds—sharp and unrelenting in their beauty.

And I trembled in his arms, afraid of what he wanted and what he offered. Afraid I wasn't worthy of him.

The water poured over us and I held him tightly while he pounded into me, and everything went bright and shiny.

Before I realized what I was doing, I was plunging my fangs into his neck.

His hot blood filled my mouth and I moaned, drinking his essence. Pure bliss exploded and my whole body felt as though it had shattered.

"Patricia!" He plunged deeply, his fingers jabbing into my thighs as he lifted his head and howled.

I woke up in Gabriel's arms, which was the best feeling ever. He kissed me good morning (you know what I mean). We were lying on a big bed in a small cave and we were under a sheet. *Naked.* This thrilled me to no end.

"Drink your breakfast," he said.

I looked at him coyly. "You like it when I sink my fangs into your neck, don't you?"

"Damn right I do."

So, I happily drank my pint and was delighted to note that Gabriel was getting hard as a rock. He was so handsome. So built. So naked. I was nearly drooling with the possibilities.

He looked me over as if I were the most enticing item on the buffet. He took me into his arms and pressed his hot mouth to mine, and I purred.

He tasted like pure sex. Oh, Lord. He cupped my breasts, thumbing my nipples into hardness. I tingled all the way to my woman parts.

He stopped kissing me and licked my lips. Oh, yeah, baby. I wiggled my tongue along the seam of his mouth and he seemed to appreciate the gesture right back.

"You are beautiful," he muttered as he leaned down and tugged a nipple into his mouth. His tongue flicked the peak. I moaned.

I caressed his cock between my palms, then grasped it with one hand, using my other to cup his balls. He had a helluva package. I can't recall ever seeing a man as big as him—at least not one who wasn't starring in a porn film.

He wasted no time exploring my nether regions and within moments, I was a squirming mess. My hands were everywhere on him, and man alive, he was all hard and muscled and . . . hmmm.

Desperation mixed with mind-numbing lust. Gabriel was surprised when I got on top of him and rubbed my wet self along the ridge of his length. I wasn't paying much attention to what he was doing because I was really close to a mondo orgasm.

He flipped me onto my back, dispelling the tight, coiling pleasure in my womb. His gold eyes were wild and seemed to have changed shape.

"I'm the alpha." He growled.

Oh, come on. Growling? He didn't scare me. Getting all particular about who was on top didn't deter me from my goal. Talking to me like that only made me hotter.

I wrapped my legs around his waist and tried to get his cock inside me.

He growled again. Something animalistic flashed in his eyes. He got up on his knees, grasping my wrists to yank me up with him. "Submit to me."

Chapter 17

I laughed. Was he joking?

Gabriel seemed nonplussed at my reaction. "Submit, Patricia."

I wrenched my wrists free of his grip; then I wrapped my hand around his cock. "Tell you what, stud. We can submit to each other or . . ."

He sucked in a sharp breath. "Or what?"

"Or I'll pull off your dick and feed it to the demons."

Startled, he stared at me. Then his lips stretched into a wicked grin. "You are definitely the one for me, Patricia."

"Tell it to my vagina." I fell backward onto the bed and nearly cried when he covered me and finally, finally, *finally* guided his thick cock inside me.

I met every thrust, moaning and mewling and acting a fool. But I didn't care. In no time at all, I plunged over the edge into sparkling bliss and then he did, too.

I should've known that happiness like this was as fleeting as a good-hair day.

When Gabriel and I got dressed and entered the main cavern, we were met by a pissed-off Terran, an indifferent Zerina, and a happy-to-see-us Arin.

I stayed close to Gabriel. He smelled yummy, like chocolate chip cookies and sex, and he felt really good, too. Y'know, being bound to him wasn't too bad.

"We've been worried sick!" yelled Terran as she marched over to Gabriel and gave him the stink-eye. "How many times have I told you to *carry your phone*?" She thrust the slim, red cell phone at him and he meekly took it.

"I thought you lost it in the woods," I said.

"I found it. I *always* find it. I'm the cleanup girl." Terran punched Gabriel in the shoulder. "Jerk."

"We have a visitor," said Arin, clearing his throat.

Patrick sat on the edge of the fountain, looking like someone had ripped out his heart.

"Jessica's missing," he said.

"He thought she was here," said Zerina. She was looking as if she wanted to push him into the pool.

"When you didn't show up at the shelter," said Patrick, "I figured you came back."

"I couldn't get in to the shelter. The blood lock wouldn't open for me." I put my hands on my hips. "So, you thought we kidnapped Jessica?"

Arin looked nonplussed. "Why would we do that?"

"I can't reach her by phone or through our mental connection," said Patrick. "Everyone else is in the compound, so I thought . . . maybe she was here."

"How's Wilson?" I asked.

"He's fine," said Patrick. "He's been helping out with the younger children. He asked if you were okay."

That made my inner mama bear roar with happiness. Gabriel draped his arm on my shoulders, a sign of comfort or possession, I didn't know. Who cared so long as his arm was around my shoulders?

"We have to help," I told him quietly. "You know how many times I cried on her shoulder or stayed at her house when my ex-husband got crazy? I can't count the number of times she took my son to the movies or for ice cream so he wouldn't have to listen to me fight with Sean. I owe her. I don't renege on my debts."

"Your debts are my debts." He kissed me. "We will save Jessica."

Patrick's phone rang. We were all startled by the sudden noise. He flipped it open and listened.

"It's just static," he said. He looked down at the display. "It's her number."

"Don't close it!" I pointed at his phone. "Maybe she's calling you, but she can't talk. Use the GPS thingie to track her location."

"The Thrifty Sip?" asked Patrick as we drove up to the abandoned convenience store. Terran owned a Hummer, of all things, which had been camouflaged in the woods. Arin stayed at the cave, which was real close to the cemetery. Patrick had pointed out that the cavern was near to where the Consortium had blown up the Wraiths.

The Thrifty Sip was a few miles from the town proper. It was also on the schedule for demolition—a security risk or some such. The compound had the only available gas station nowadays.

I didn't have a car. Sean took ours when I told him it was over and I hadn't been able to afford another one. Sometimes, I caught a ride with others, but mostly I walked to where I wanted to go. I got to places a whole lot faster after becoming a vampire.

We all piled out of the huge gas-guzzler and stared at the empty, dark building. I turned to Patrick. "Is she in there?"

"No," said Patrick. "She's right here."

I didn't want to second-guess him, even though I was dying to say something along the lines of, "Are you sure you know how to read a GPS?"

Everyone looked around. It was quiet and dark. Nothing and no one stirred.

"Spread out," commanded Terran. "We'll check a hundred feet in every direction and meet back here."

I touched Patrick's elbow. "Is your mind-mojo working yet?"

"No. I can't sense her at all."

While Terran barked orders, the rest of us walked down the road in both directions, behind the store, into the little pocket of woods nearby, and across the ditch to the empty field.

Jessica wasn't here.

We met back at the Thrifty Sip. Patrick looked about ready to spit nails. "Where the bloody hell is my wife?" Patrick ran a hand through his hair. "I'm sorry."

"I understand," said Gabriel. "I would feel the same if it were Patsy who'd been taken."

"Would you?" asked Patrick. "Because of the prophecy?"

"Hey, now," I interrupted. "Let's not forget all the crap you put Jessica through going on about your *sonuachar*."

Patrick had the grace to look abashed.

"Is it just me, or does the air stink like testosterone?" asked Zerina. Gabriel sent his gold glare to the girl. She didn't care. "Maybe Jessica would appreciate being found. Ya think?"

"The GPS pinpointed this location," insisted Patrick.

"Maybe we need to look down," said Zerina. She was dressed in a pink shirt, black jeans, and black leather ankle boots. She stomped on the circle of metal under her boot.

"Aw, hell," I muttered. "She's somewhere in the sewer."

* * *

When Zerina pulled off the manhole cover, Patrick jumped the forty or so feet into the sewer line. Then Terran dropped into the hole. We heard one big splash and I flinched. The stink rising up from the manhole, especially to all of us with overdeveloped senses, was dis-*gus*-ting.

Well, if everyone else could stand swimming around in it, I guess I could, too. I just couldn't guarantee I wouldn't yak.

Gabriel climbed down on the metal ladder that extended down into the dark, smelly space. Then I went. Zerina stayed topside to be the lookout.

Gabriel splashed into the water (yuck, yuck, yuck). It was waist-high on him. He waded to the side where there was a small concrete ledge that wound alongside the sewer water. I nearly died from the stench, but I remembered that I could fly, too.

So I drifted down the hole and over the nasty water. I stepped onto the ledge.

Terran asked, "Do you still have the Glock?"

"Er . . . it sorta got blown up in my trailer." It seemed like that had happened years ago instead of just days.

"Don't worry, Terran," said Gabriel. "Patricia can handle herself."

Patrick did some clever things with his hands and muttered Gaelic. Glowing orbs filled the air.

Patrick flew about two feet above the water, staying between those of us walking.

Jessica was flattened against a wall on the left side, pinned through the shoulders with metal stakes. Each thigh had a stake through it, too.

She was unconscious.

The ungodly sound that issued from Patrick made every hair stand up on my body. Whoever had done this to his wife was going to pay with their lives.

We all ran toward her.

Patrick got there first. He grabbed the metal stake in her left shoulder and Gabriel grabbed the one in her right. Terran and I knelt to get the ones in her thighs. We all pulled with every bit of our supernatural strength.

Not one budged.

"Bespelled?" asked Terran, panting.

Poor Jess' clothes were black with her blood. She was still blindfolded, too. Whoever had done this to her was cruel. They didn't want to kill her. They wanted to torment her.

"We need Zela," said Patrick.

"You're the only one who can get to her the fastest," said Gabriel. "We won't leave your mate."

Patrick nodded, and then he sparkled out of sight. While he was gone, the rest of us kept pulling on the ugly spikes.

God, Jess looked pale. Beyond vampire pale. And there was so much blood. I couldn't begin to imagine the kind of pain that had consumed her when they drove those stakes into her body.

When Patrick returned, he was alone. "She's on the way," he said.

"What the hell is going on?"

I heard Jessica's voice, so I looked up. Her eyes were closed and her mouth wasn't moving.

Oh, no.

The spirit of Jessica stood next to her body.

I saw a thin silver line that connected her spirit to her physical form. If that chain broke, she would be free of this life for good. And then we would lose Patrick, too.

Jessica kept talking to Patrick, hands on her hips, her expression pure pissed off.

"Jess."

She looked down at me. "Could you tell my stubborn husband that ignoring his wife is a no-nookie offense?"

"Honey, you're . . ." I couldn't finish the sentence. She didn't know she was a wandering spirit.

Patrick reached over and grabbed my shoulders. "Please," he said in a broken voice. "Do not tell me you see my wife. She is *not* dead."

Chapter 18

"I'm dead? You mean, *dead*-dead?" Jessica smacked herself in the forehead with her palm. "Duh. Only you can see me. Of course, I am. Damn! This sucks." She turned around and examined her staked body. "Wow. I look awful."

"You're not dead, Jess. You're just having an out-of-body experience. You have to stay real close to yourself until it's time to get you back in there."

"Okay." She looked down and saw Gabriel. "Hey, is that your wolfie? He's hot. When Patrick started in with all that soul mate crap, I really wanted to punch him in the mouth. But he was right." She smiled at me. "Does Gabriel make you happy? Do you go all gooey when he looks at you or touches you?"

"Yeah," I said. "On all counts."

"What's she saying?" asked Patrick.

"She thinks Gabriel is hot." The laugh burbling in my throat turned to a sob. Gabriel looked at me, sympathy glowing in his eyes. He was still kneeling at Jessica's thigh, his hands gripping the metal.

"You're definitely talking to Jessica."

"Nobody's hotter than he is," said Jess, grinning. "He's the hottest of the hotties."

"She says you're the hottest of all."

Patrick tried for a smile, but didn't quite make it. "I will see you soon, *mo chroi*. I love you."

"Isn't he sweet?" Jessica cupped his face, though of course he didn't know it. "Tell him I said 'back at you, babe.'"

"She loves you, too."

Passing along messages between spirits and people was a tiresome thing. And Jessica liked to jaw on more than anyone else I knew.

"How did they get you?"

Jessica looked embarrassed. "I went back to our house to check on the stupid pony. Jenny was worried about Glitter. I took a digital camera so I could take pictures and show her the horse was all right." She shrugged. "I guess they figured I was better than no hostage at all."

"She snuck out to check on Glitter. She figures the bad guys saw it as an opportunity to strike."

Patrick's anguish was palpable. "She should've told me."

"She knows that," I said. "She's sorry."

"Wow, Pats. You're good. So, what's the plan of attack?" asked Jessica. (See what I mean?) "Y'know, for getting me back into my body?"

"We're waiting on Zela," I said.

"Oh," said Jessica. "She's the one who has the metal mojo."

"We need information about Koschei or we might all find ourselves staked to walls." Terran's voice was no-nonsense.

"Gah! Who's the bitch?" Jessica's words had no heat to them. She waved away her own rancor. "She's right. Koschei is behind this whole thing. Man, that guy is such a dickhead."

"She says Koschei is a dickhead."

"We are aware of his personality," said Terran, whose lips tugged into a reluctant smile. "We need to know his plan."

"Well, he didn't exactly tell me, now did he?

He's a helluva lot scarier than Ron. Anyhoodles, the only other thing I know is that they have a real hankering to raise the dead. Is that gross, or what?"

"What is she saying?" asked Terran impatiently.

"She says Koschei has been busy recruiting other vampires to his cause. And that he's raising an army of zombies."

At that moment a woman arrived. She was statuesque and cocoa-skinned, and very well dressed. Her silver hoop earrings jangled as she assessed Jessica's staked body.

"Move away," she said in a thick, exotic accent. "I need space to do this work."

"Jess, this is your ride back to consciousness," I said, as we all fell back. "At least, I think it is. Stay close. You'll know when it's time to go back in."

Jessica nodded. Her gaze went to Patrick, who stubbornly stayed right where he was. This did not disturb Zela. "When I have freed her from the metal, you must catch her."

Patrick nodded, his expression grim.

Spirit Jessica stood between her body and Patrick, her ghostly arms clasped around his neck.

Zela turned her hand up and pointed it at the

metal stake in Jess' left shoulder. She clenched a fist and the spike jerked out of the wall and hovered. She put her palm down and it clattered to the concrete.

"How the hell can she do that?" I asked.

"Her Family power is the ability to control metals of any kind," said Patrick.

Zela worked her magic three more times and Jessica flopped forward. Patrick grabbed her and held on tightly. I watched her spirit rejoin her body. Relief cascaded through me.

Patrick scooped Jessica into his arms and sparkled out of the chamber.

Zela stepped forward and offered her hand. I took it. Power surged through me. "It is done," she said. She lowered her head. "My queen."

"Er . . . thanks." It figured I'd gained the last of the seven powers of the Ancients in a sewer.

A scream echoed.

"Zerina," whispered Terran.

All of us ran toward the entrance, even the Ancients, though they had the power to leave.

Zerina plummeted through the manhole, her body flailing as she hit the nasty water. She didn't come back up.

Fire whooshed down from the manhole. The huge wave of flame rushed toward us.

Everything happened so fast. Zela grabbed Terran, who was closest to her, and in a flash, they were gone, out of danger's way.

In the blink of an eye, Zela returned and reached for me, but Gabriel was between us. I pushed him into her arms and they disappeared, both horrified by what I'd done. Hey, if I was the queen, then I got to say who freaking got saved.

The only thing I could do was jump into the water. I tried not to think about what I was swimming through. I just kept under the muck and moved away from the manhole. I didn't have to breathe, so it made getting the hell out of there much easier.

When I finally broke the surface, the flame was gone. I wasn't sure what to do next. Find another way out?

I climbed onto the ledge and thought about which way to go. I was disoriented and unsure of how far I'd gone.

I crept down the ledge toward the manhole, hoping that Lia and whoever else might be up there were gone. I couldn't decide if I should try to get up on that ladder and escape, or try using my new powers.

Then I heard splashing and froze. Zerina poked through the dark water. Her pink eyes darted around the tunnel and found me, a quivering mess, huddled against the wall.

"Did everyone get out?" she asked. She swam toward the ledge and hoisted herself up.

"Seeing as I'm the only one not gone, then yeah, you could assume everyone of importance got out."

She grinned at me. "Don't get your panties in a wad, Patsy. Why do you think I screamed and fell into the water?"

"You did it on purpose?"

She squeezed out her shirt and brown water dribbled onto the pavement. Yuck. "Stupid Koschei sent a minion from the Family Hua. No matter how good you are at mind-screwing, you can't get that slightly glazed look out of your victim's eyes." She shook her head. "Besides, I'm a fairy. You can't glamour me. I wished I hadn't gone for the big splash."

Oh, yeah. She was Sidhe. She could fly.

"So, you're sure it wasn't Lia who sent the fire down here?"

"Nah. Lia would've fried me on site." She looked down at her ruined outfit. "This stuff reeks. Humans are disgusting."

I could agree with her since I wasn't a human. Nausea swished in my stomach. The smell was getting to me. I looked at the ladder. "I guess we'd better get out of here."

"Why'd they put the ladder in the middle like that? You *have* to go into the sewage!" complained Zerina.

Good question. But not one I could answer.

Zerina walked off the ledge and floated in the air. She looked back at me and waited with pink eyebrows raised.

"I'm all out of magic dust," said Zerina sweetly. "Let's go, queenie. I smell like manure-filled, sweaty socks."

I rolled my eyes. I'd flown down here. I could fly out of here, too. I thought about flying, told myself I could fly, and stepped off the ledge.

And dropped like a stone into the sewer water.

Zerina's laughter pealed like church bells.

"Oh, shut up," I groused as I swam toward the ladder. This time, I imagined floating upward, and within seconds, I was rising out of the water.

Zerina insisted on going up first, and who was I to argue with a pink fairy? She poked her head through the hole. After a few seconds of looking around, she climbed out.

I followed.

We headed toward the Hummer, which the minion had thoughtfully not blown up.

"What's that?" I asked, pointing toward town. A huge red bubble bumped against the night sky. "That's where the compound is."

My stomach cramped and I bent over. I pressed a palm against my tummy and wished I had the ability to take deep, calming breaths.

"Fuck," said Zerina, yanking open the driver's-side door. "That's the work of demons."

By the time we got to the cave, we were both a mess. Me, because I was feeling sick. Zerina, because we were stinking up Terran's pride and joy so much she was gonna kill us.

Zerina got us into the hidey-hole the same way Terran had. When we stumbled into the cavern, Arin was pacing and pulling at the hair on his head.

"You're all right!" he cried, hurrying toward us. He stopped short and slapped a hand against his nose and mouth. "You smell like—"

"Shit," Zerina and I said together. I didn't care about the fancy couches. I plopped onto one and squeezed my eyes shut. "That's how I feel, too."

"You feel that way because you're separated from Gabriel," said Arin. "That's the way it works with life mates."

"Vampires, too," I muttered. "But I didn't think it would be like this."

"You ladies must bathe." Arin backed away, waving his hand in front of his face. "Then we will discuss the plan to free the others."

My eyes popped open. "Does this have something to do with the demon bubble?"

"The Consortium evacuated everyone into the shelter beneath the compound," said Arin. "They're trapped."

Amahté

Translated from the Memoirs of Ruadan

Amahté was the high priest of Anubis and a favorite of Pharaoh Amenemhet II. He brought offerings to Anubis and cared for his shrine. Anubis rewarded his faithful service. The god gave him the ability to speak to the dead and he also gave him the ability to raise the dead.

He was a tall man with a shaved head and always wore a white garment that looped over one shoulder.

I became friends with him and his family. One night, I went to meet Amahté and found him outside the temple, bleeding from a slit throat. Later, I learned that jealous rivals had attacked him.

"My friend! It is me, Ruadan. We have talked much these last few nights, remember?"

Amahté's eyes clearly showed that he did.

"I can save you. But my gift has a price. You will not be able to see the sun again, my friend, but you will live forever. You will be among those I have chosen to rule our kind. Do you accept my offer?"

Amahté took an inordinate amount of time to decide. Blood seeped from between his fingers and pooled blackly on the ground. Finally, he managed a weak nod.

Here is where I will describe the process for Turning. The first six vampires required seven symbols. Turning others requires only the symbol of the Family.

I removed Amahté's hands from the wound. The blood poured out. I watched the life drain from my friend.

Amahté lay still, his caramel skin going gray, his eyes wide and unstaring. I muttered the spells over Amahté, pressing my palms against his chest.

After I secured Amahté's soul, I removed a small, gold knife tucked into his wide belt. I punctured my forefinger and rubbed it on Amahté's neck wound.

The skin started to mend.

Then I carved symbols into Amahté's flesh: one on each wrist; one on the top of each foot; one on the forehead; one on the chest; and one on the belly.

I pierced my finger again and with my blood, I retraced all the symbols I'd cut into Amahté. As I did so, they all glowed gold.

I slit my wrist and pressed it against the lips of the man I hoped to save.

Amahté began to drink.

Minutes passed, but it felt like years when I finally pulled his wrist away.

Amahté's body started to convulse. His eyes rolled into the back of his head and his arms and legs went wild. The symbols went bright white and Amahté screamed.

He went still. The symbols burned into his skin. The blackened marks faded slowly, until they couldn't be seen anymore.

I finished my gruesome work. Blood splattered the man on the ground, staining his white clothes. I fared no better—my own clothing was soiled with his blood.

I found a deep, dark cave to hide in. When we awoke, Amahté insisted on seeing his family. He thought it better they believe him dead. However, he refused to leave Egypt.

His son, Khenti, was already full grown. Not

long after his father became *deamhan fola*, Khenti became a high priest.

He met the same fate as his father. As Khenti lay dying from stab wounds, Amahté came to him and Turned him.

Amahté was the fifth vampire I Turned. He refused to leave Egypt with me, but agreed to be on the Council and to attend the meeting with the others. I was restless and decided to leave the lands of the Nile.

I headed north once again and crossed the water until I reached what is now called Italy.

Chapter 19

"Why not blow up the compound?" asked Zerina. "Why keep them trapped?"

I heard multiple screams and jerked upright. Zerina and Arin glanced at me and I realized I was the only one hearing the cries. The spirits in this cave were lamenting, but good. What Zerina had said upset them mightily.

Arin was looking green. "Please. For the love of heaven. Go shower. A lot. Then we'll talk."

Zerina and I went to the cave with its waterfall. We got undressed and stood under the cold water until the smell went away.

My clothes were beyond help. Zerina was too

small and Arin too thin to offer anything to wear, so they dug through Terran's stuff. She liked leather, and I liked comfort, so nothing there, either. Besides, she was short and lithe. I was tall and had boobs to spare.

"Hang on," said Zerina. She wove her hands in the air. Pink sparkles zipped back and forth. After a few minutes, she offered me the most gorgeous blue dress I'd ever seen. It fit perfectly and flowed around me like spun silk. I wasn't much of a dress fan, but I loved this one.

"The fabric is woven from fairy magic, so it'll protect you. Plus, that color matches your eyes."

"Thanks, Zee." I hugged her, which she hated.

She pushed out of my arms. "Get away from me. Sheesh!"

Shoes were a problem, so I went barefoot. I'd given myself a nice little pedicure a few nights before, so my shiny red toes didn't look half bad. I wrung out my wet hair as best I could and then borrowed hairpins from Terran's stash. I put my hair into a simple updo just to keep it out of my face.

And that was as good as I was gonna get.

Arin had disposed of the couch I'd sat on and sprayed some kind of smell-good stuff in the air.

All the same, I caught a whiff of sewer every now and again.

We told Arin about everything that happened and he sat back on the couch with his arms behind his head, thinking hard.

"*Everyone* is in the bubble?" I asked. "You don't think they're . . . hurting anyone, do you? My son is in there. All the kids are!"

Gabriel and Terran were there, too. Where else would Zela take them?

My fear for Wilson and Gabriel was so great, I wanted to leave that moment and take a tire iron to that demon barricade. *Please, God,* I prayed again, *help him. Help us all!*

"They're trapped," said Arin. "I suspect the demons were forced to erect the barrier. Koschei couldn't know who had gone into the sewer. Though they probably suspected Zela had, which is why they made sure only she could remove the stakes. Getting rid of Patrick and Jessica would be a boon, too."

Something niggled my mind. I couldn't quite catch it. Then it snapped to the front and I gasped. "We don't know what will happen to a Family if the Ancient dies. That's why the others are trying to figure out ways to capture Koschei without killing him."

"Why would Koschei care about what happened to Zela or her Family? He could wipe out a whole contingent at once. Maybe he was hoping to see what would happen if an Ancient died."

Arin's logic was scary. Come to think of it, so was Koschei's. Waves of nausea forced me to close my eyes for a second. I got all dizzy and felt faint, so I opened them again.

"All right, what's the plan?" Feeling like I was gonna puke any second made me cranky.

"As far as we know, there are only the three of us," said Arin. He looked at me speculatively. "You say that you have all seven powers?"

"Yes." I got up and paced, hoping the sickness would go away. Fat chance. I was missing Gabriel something fierce. "I don't mind using any of 'em except the demon mojo."

Zerina shook her head. "Good call. Demons don't like to be bossed around. If you lose control for a second, they'll rip out your heart and eat it while you die right in front of 'em."

"Nice." I felt dizzy again, so I sat down.

"To make demons do a spell that big," continued Zerina, "means at least ten vamps are using their powers together."

"How the hell are we going to beat them?" I sat back and tried deep breathing. My lungs hadn't worked properly since the day I died and they refused my request to operate. I couldn't remember if I'd had my pint. I seemed hungry. Sorta. Ever have that feeling of being starved, but you know if you ate a thing, you'd just barf it back up? Well, that was me, all right.

"You don't look well," said Zerina, frowning.

"I need Gabriel," I admitted.

For a moment, we all sat there, lost in our thoughts, not feeling all that hopeful.

After a minute or two, I got the feeling of being watched. I looked up into the gaunt face of a girl. She was dressed in black, with kohled eyes and red lips.

"Please," she said softly. "Can you help us?"

I looked around the ghosts encircling the cave. "You're one of them?"

She nodded. "Can you release us from this place?"

"I don't know," I answered honestly. "Why are all of you stuck here to begin with? That's a lot of souls with unfinished business."

"Those Consortium assholes blew us up," said another voice from the shadows.

When we first got Turned, Jessica had been kidnapped by Ron, who was then leader of the Wraiths. He had died of the Taint, but not before he used his own followers to conduct experiments. Honestly, I was fuzzy on what had happened during her rescue.

"Ron told us to prepare for battle," she said. "But no one showed up to fight. We were confused, running around in this mist that came outta nowhere. Ron escaped, but left most of us behind in the cave.

"The whole place filled with light. As if the sun had escaped its orbit and rolled on through the cave. We all died."

I met the concerned looks of Zerina and Arin. Well, mostly Arin. Zerina was tucked onto her favorite divan, looking at her pile of books.

"What's going on?" he asked.

I rubbed my forehead. "Jessica was kidnapped by the Wraiths a few months ago. After she was rescued, a few of the Masters blew up the Wraiths who'd been hiding out in a cave."

That's when I realized we were in the same area. No wonder Gabriel and his crew had managed to get inside the borders and hide in here. This whole place was off-limits, especially to the Turn-bloods.

All the same, I looked at my newest ghost pal. "This isn't the cave that collapsed."

"It's nearby. We saw your psychic energy. We were drawn here." She knelt and placed a translucent hand on my knee. "You must help us."

Since they'd once been Wraiths, and therefore surely subscribed to the belief that vampires should be the top of the food chain, I wasn't too keen on helping them do anything.

I looked at the girl. "I'll try."

"Thank you," she said. She returned to the ranks of the dead watching me from the perimeter. Creepy.

"The ghosts of the Wraiths are here?" asked Arin. He sounded horrified.

"The good news just keeps coming, doesn't it?" I sighed. You know what? I may feel like I had the worst case of flu ever, but I was not helpless. I could command ghosts. I could also wield the seven powers of the Ancients.

I got off the couch and found a clear space. I knelt down and held my arms up, palms out as Khenti had taught me. I whispered the words of magic he'd given me. Above me, a portal of pure white light opened.

"Only your fears and confusion hold you here," I said to the ghosts. "If you want freedom, go to the Light."

I heard their murmurs, felt their doubts, but there was nothing for them here. A few moved into the portal . . . and then a few more. The trickle turned into a flood and within minutes, all the souls had left the cave.

As the girl with kohled eyes stepped into the heavenly light, she smiled. "Thanks."

The gate closed behind her.

Wow.

I got to my feet and returned to the couch. Arin and Zerina were staring at me, their mouths hanging open.

"What?" I asked. "I opened a portal and sent about a hundred ghosts through it."

"It feels different in here," said Arin. "Lighter. Not as . . . depressing."

"Yeah, well, Wraiths aren't exactly cheerful creatures." My icky-sick feeling had returned. I wanted Gabriel here more than anything. I missed him. I felt like I was missing half my body. He made me whole. Corny, but there you have it.

Nonna and Dottie had done a good job of staying out of my way, which was unlike them. But now, I needed them. "Nonna, Dottie, come to me now!"

In the blink of an eye, my friends popped into sight. They floated in front of me, looking highly annoyed. I rolled my eyes. "What? Did I interrupt you watching the Food Network on some other person's TV?"

"No," said Nonna.

"Me and your granny had a meeting," said Dottie. "And we decided you were right."

"You guys have meetings?" I couldn't fathom them going off by themselves and chatting over ghost tea and cookies. I squinted at them, suspicious. "And just what is it I'm right about?"

"Being more useful." Dottie pulled out her Pall Malls. For once, it didn't bother me that she was smoking. Being a reluctant nonsmoker was the least of my worries. "We've been spying."

"On who?"

"We went along to that Kosher's place," said Dottie. "He's holed up near the cemetery."

"So are we. And his name is Koschei."

"Whatever. He's way on the other side of it. Him and that Lia are loony tunes, if you ask me."

No kiddin'.

"You're really pissing him off," continued Dottie.

"He's lost his soul and his patience," cracked Nonna. She giggled at her own joke. "They got lots of vampires and werewolves and other creatures."

"Lycans have joined them?" This was worse than I thought. Koschei was definitely going for more than the rule-the-vamps angle.

"Joined who?" asked Arin.

I waved away his question. "I need you two to go to the shelter and tell me if everyone is okay. Check on Wil and Gabriel."

But Dottie was shaking her head as she poured out a stream of smoke. "No can do, hon. We've already tried. Thought you were there, you see. We wanted to report in." She looked at me, sympathy glowing in her eyes. "That's some nasty shit, Pats. Nothing can get through that barrier. Not even ghosts."

Chapter 20

After I relayed all the information Dottie and Nonna had told me, Arin went to his desk to look up stuff about demons.

I lay down on the couch, but changing position did nothing to alleviate how sick I felt. "You know, I have Durga's powers. Why couldn't I go and work some of my own demon magic?"

Of course, the only experience I had with bossing around demons was when I told one demon to go to hell. Well, wasn't I the foretold queen of vampires and lycans? Surely, I could kick some butt.

I missed Gabriel. And not just because I

wanted to puke up my guts because he wasn't around.

My stomach squeezed and burbled. What I wouldn't give for an Alka-Seltzer. "Maybe Gabriel isn't in the shelter." I looked up at Dottie and Nonna. "Would you try to find him, please?"

They looked at each other, shrugged, and then pop—*poof*, they were gone.

Arin returned to where we were sitting. The fountain trickled happily. Funny how beautiful things like statues with trickling water had no worth when you were looking at the end of your life, and the lives of your friends. I was beginning to see why the dead were not overly concerned with big events. What did it matter? Dead was dead.

"If Koschei's hideout is nearby," said Arin, "maybe we should hit him directly."

"You really think we can sneak into Koschei's place?" I asked. I hated to say it, but I was feeling a little outgunned. Strangely enough, I was also starting to feel better. Maybe lying down had done the trick.

Or maybe . . . Hope shot through me. Was Gabriel on his way here?

Dottie appeared suddenly and danced around the fountain, excited. "We found Gabriel!"

I sat up and jumped off the couch. "You did? Where is he?"

"Close," said Nonna as she floated next to me. "Looks hurt. And that girl he's with—"

But the three of us were in motion. Zerina led the way to the secret exit. This time she created earthen stairs for us to climb.

Nonna was right. Gabriel was just a few feet away.

But he wasn't in his human form.

He was the white wolf.

His fur was soaked in blood. He was panting hard and walking slowly. On his back, he carried an unconscious and bloodied Terran.

"Gabriel!" I dove to my knees and wrapped my arms around his big, furry neck. "Are you okay?" I kissed his jaw, his ear, his nose.

He whined, nuzzling me.

Arin gently lifted Terran from Gabriel's back. He carried her to the entrance. Zerina followed, looking more upset than I'd ever seen her. Nonna and Dottie were pleased as punch with themselves.

I held on to Gabriel's thick fur and dry-wept. I was so glad to see him. So glad he was okay. So glad we were together.

After we were all safely in the tunnel, Zerina sealed the entrance.

"It's getting close to dawn," I said. "I don't have any control over when I pass out. Luckily, that's the same for all vampires, Ancients or not."

Arin placed Terran on the couch. He looked at me. "That's true. And it may be why Koschei has gathered guardians and other creatures to him."

"Still, it might be easier to breach his security during the day," said Zerina, kneeling next to Terran. She wiped off the blood encrusting Terran's arms. "These are bite marks. Gabriel, were you attacked by lycans?"

He barked, which I took to mean yes. "Dottie, Nonna, can you go spy some more at Koschei's?"

"Damn straight." Dottie saluted smartly. Nonna did the same, grinning widely.

They disappeared.

"Come on, baby," I said to Gabriel. "Let's get you cleaned up."

We walked to the cave with its wonderful waterfall. I got undressed while Gabriel got human. I didn't want to get my new dress soiled, especially since it was the only garment I currently owned.

I wasn't real keen on watching the morphing process. The crunch of bones realigning was hard on my eardrums, not to mention all the changing of fur to skin.

Gabriel sat, naked and bloody and weary, on the floor of the cave. I knelt down and cupped his face. "Are you all right?"

"I thought I'd lost you," he whispered. His golden eyes held tears. "As soon as Zela dumped us at the shelter, we got the hell out of there."

"But the demon barrier . . ."

"We're lycans," he said. "We dug under it. Unfortunately, we ran into the lycans protecting the vampires—the ones casting the demon spells. Terran got the worst of it."

"She'll be okay," I said, not knowing if it was true. She looked bad. "I'm just glad you made it back alive."

He stood under the waterfall and I helped him wash away the grime and blood. Then I scooped up my dress and we walked to the cave with its comfy bed.

Gabriel and I fell asleep in each other's arms.

Terran appeared in the doorway and cleared her throat.

I yanked my fangs free of Gabriel's prime flesh. The holes sealed up almost immediately. I wiped the blood off his skin. Damn! I was hoping to get some nookie before the end of the world.

"It's good to see you standing on your own two feet," said Gabriel, grinning.

Terran's expression was caught between amusement and annoyance.

Boom! The earth shook all around us.

"Koschei's attacking," said Terran. "You two might want to get dressed."

I felt like I was Maid Marian joining Robin Hood and the Merry Men as they snuck through Sherwood Forest, especially barefoot and in my fairy blue dress. Hey, I've seen the movie, okay? I'm not a complete dunce.

The plan was simple: I would raise a zombie army and use 'em against the bad guys. Hopefully, we'd distract the others long enough to destroy the demon shield. Nyah, nyah!

We could see the demon shield was up and running, but it was fluctuating badly. The vampires in the compound were probably giving them hell.

I kept praying that everyone there was okay. And that Wilson wasn't freaking out. The sooner we defeated Koschei, the sooner I'd get to see my son.

Gabriel and I would stay in the cemetery and

rouse the corpses (ugh). Arin, Zerina, and Terran would go to the compound and cause all kinds of trouble for the bad guys surrounding the barrier. I wasn't sure how it would work out with the demon angle. I had a hard enough time with the ghosts.

Gabriel and I stayed at the edge of the forest. Dottie and Nonna floated above the treetops, keeping a lookout for us. Terran and the others took off for the Hummer. Why not ride to the war in style?

"Are you scared?" asked Gabriel, holding my hand.

"Terrified," I admitted. "How about you?"

"I'm the alpha," he said. "I'm never scared."

"Liar, liar, pants on fire." I kissed him soundly. Then we crept from the protection of the woods and into the cemetery.

Khenti had hammered the process into my mind during our little session. I got on my hands and knees, placed my palms on the ground, and said, "Rise!"

I'm sorry if you're disappointed in the how-to here. I wasn't all that impressed myself. But I wasn't going to argue with a four-thousand-year-old vampire or ask him to make it fancier just to impress anyone watching me.

Energy poured from my hands into the

ground. The yellow light emitting from my palms felt hot and zappy, like lightning.

The ground rumbled ominously.

The whole cemetery shook as if an earthquake were ravaging its sleeping residents. The grave nearest to us burst open and a rotting coffin plopped onto the grass.

The lid flew off and a pair of wrinkled arms extended up. The embalmed corpse sat up and looked at me. Well, sorta. Her eyes weren't open. (Y'know, because she didn't have any. Ugh!) But that wasn't the worst thing.

My very first zombie was the dead body of my grandmother.

Chapter 21

"Would you look at that!" Nonna flew around her corpse. "I look just like I did when I died."

"I told you we buried you in the pink dress. See?"

She was nodding happily. "And I'm wearing my wedding ring, too. Oh, and the gold cross my mother gave to me on my thirteenth birthday."

I had never seen anyone as thrilled to see their own dead body as my grandmother. Actually, I'd never seen *anyone* thrilled when faced with the proof of their own demise.

Poppa burst out of his coffin. He'd died ten years before Nonna. My ghost grandma actually tried to straighten his tie. "It's not really him," I hissed. "Stop that!"

"He never could tie a knot properly."

"He didn't tie that one for sure," I pointed out. I stood up and dusted off my dirty hands. "He was *dead*."

"Well, your father never could tie worth a damn, either."

I rolled my eyes. My parents had requested to be cremated and I was thankful for that. I didn't think I could face the shuffling dead feet of my grandparents *and* my parents. Good Lord.

All throughout the cemetery, coffins were bursting from the ground like demented daisies on an ugly spring day. Whatever occupied the coffin crawled out, and I was surprised to see skeletons as well as deteriorating carcasses and the embalmed.

"I'm going to hell," I said. "I've just desecrated more than a hundred years worth of Broken Heart dead."

"I don't mind," said Nonna. "I can't wait to see me kick ass."

Getting zombies to move fast, much less as a unit, was not easy. If something obstructed the walking dead, they just marched in place instead of trying to find a way around it. I understood now why Khenti said they were puppets. They couldn't think. They were only in motion because of me.

Some of them were really disgusting. The smell was worse than what we endured in the sewer, but I wasn't complaining. I felt much braver going to face Koschei, even if my new recruits weren't exactly up to snuff.

I don't know how many of Broken Heart's undead we had marching along (well, they were trying to, at any rate), but it was in the hundreds. In recent times, a lot of citizens had buried their relatives in Tulsa graveyards or seen to arrangements in other states.

After what seemed like ten hours, but was really only one, we were finally approaching the compound.

At the edge of the entrance to the compound, I saw Durga with her hands facing the demon shield. I could see her lips moving, but we weren't close enough to hear the words.

I was outraged that she'd chosen the side of evil. What was wrong with these people?

A sleek gray wolf shot past us. He bounded across the field and knocked down Durga.

"Arin," said Gabriel proudly.

The demon shield wobbled like a bowl of melting Jell-O. Then it vanished. Several black shadows appeared where the dome had been, then dissipated. If those things were the demons, I hoped they'd gone back to hell. Broken Heart had enough problems, thank you.

The wolf sat on Durga's chest, his jaw clamped on her throat. She wasn't moving an inch. She needed her voice to call to her demons, and there was no way she was talking with a wolf's teeth embedded in her neck.

Gabriel and I walked to the prone Durga. Her eyes were wide and fear-filled. She probably hadn't contemplated her death in four thousand years.

"You are banned," I said softly. Gabriel joined hands with me and magic flowed from our palms. "We cast you into the world-between-worlds, Durga the Ancient."

Arin climbed off the woman and sat on his haunches, watching as Durga slowly faded. Gabriel and I stood up together.

One bad guy down.

People poured out of the compound.

Now the battle began in earnest.

Fireballs whizzed through the air. Screams and growls issued from all directions.

"Wheee! Look at me!" The body of Nonna

jogged toward me, the arms flopping crazily and the neck lolling. It whirled around, then bowed in front of me.

"What the fuck?" I scurried backward and stared at the animated corpse.

"Watch your language!" chided Nonna. But her lips weren't moving.

"Oh. My. God. Nonna! You've *possessed* your own body?"

"You were the one bellyaching about how slow going it was," said Nonna. "At least you got two recruits who can get their butts moving."

"Yeah, we're a pair." Dottie's voice issued from Poppa as he ambled up next to Nonna. They grabbed each other's arms and did a wild dance.

"Out of all the corpses you could choose, you picked Poppa?"

"It was her idea," said Dottie.

I was speechless. Gabriel put his hands on my shoulders and rubbed them until I relaxed. "Okay. Um, stay close. And pay attention. And remember you're in corporeal form, okay? You can't pass through walls or anything."

They nodded, then walked ahead of us. The other zombies continued shuffling forward. I made sure no one was trapped behind a tree stump or car or had tripped on a blade of grass, and then I moved through the swaying bodies. Gabriel caught hold of my hand, and just that little gesture made me feel so much better.

Patsy. You've done well, my minion. Come to me. And bring your army of the dead. They are exactly what I need.

"Minion, my ass," I yelled.

"Patricia?" Gabriel looked at me, his eyes flashing with fear.

I fought off Koschei's glamour, but he was strong and he had more experience. All the same, that bastard was *not* getting into my head.

Without my direction, my army of the dead was going all over the place. Zombies were running into each other, falling down and getting trodden on, and going off in opposite directions.

Y'know, zombies just didn't seem like effective fighting tools.

I pushed Koschei out of my head and slammed shut the gates to my mind. I couldn't see him. Not yet. But I knew he would find me.

Lycans fought other lycans. Vampires sought to destroy their kindred. I saw the pink hair of Zerina as she moved among a group of battling creatures I didn't recognize.

This was Broken Heart. This was the place where we wanted to create a place of peace and hope for parakind. And yet, here we all were clawing each other to bits.

I'd had enough.

Power surged through me. I felt all seven gifts of the Ancients intertwine and pulse from my fingertips all the way to my toes.

"Gabriel," I said. "It's time."

While he took his wolf form, I directed my zombies to attack our enemies. It didn't matter if they succeeded. Causing confusion among those fighting was just as useful.

Koschei appeared at the edge of the battle-field. His gaze was directly on mine, but he couldn't get into my head anymore.

The waves of fighting men and women who dared get in his way were flung into the air. He didn't care if they were friend or foe.

It was as if the darkness itself parted for him as he walked toward me. He strode arrogantly forward, his eyes gleaming with the insanity born of *droch fola*.

I stayed where I was, allowing him to come to me. In my left hand, I cupped a pure ball of energy. My other hand was on the furry head of my husband, the white wolf.

Koschei stopped a couple of feet away.

My nonna marched her body right up to him

and slugged him in the mouth. God, I loved that old lady.

Koschei reared back, obviously flummoxed that he'd been assaulted by a grandmotherly corpse.

Dottie had taken to tormenting Koschei, too. My poppa's hands were socking him in the backside, but none too effectively. I don't think Dottie or Nonna remembered much about operating a human body.

I heard the roar-squawk about a second before the dragon swooped out of the sky. Koschei escaped his two attackers and backed away, smirking.

Lia made a bow of fire. She notched two flaming arrows and shot them toward Nonna and Poppa.

Thwump. Thwump. The bodies jerked around, then fell to the ground.

Screeching, Nonna and Dottie jumped out of the burning bodies. They hopped around as if they were on fire, realized they weren't, and then stared down at the fiery corpses.

Lia laughed (why do evildoers always laugh?). She pulled on the dragon's reins and it banked right.

I threw the energy ball at the underside of its belly. White light exploded. It shrieked in pain, and rolled through the air. Lia screamed as she tried to get her pet under control.

Gabriel, my knight in white fur, stayed at my side. No one approached me. Most were too busy fighting each other or knocking over zombies.

Koschei, in the meanwhile, was doing something else. I couldn't understand the words he spouted, but I began to understand their intent when other vampires gathered behind him.

Gabriel and I stood as one. I felt energy pulse between us. The binding made us strong; love made us stronger. Prophecy or not, my place was with him. And there was no other place I wanted to be.

As we advanced on Koschei and his minions, I saw Ruadan, Patrick, and Lorcan fly over the group. They landed next to us. A sword of pure light shot out from Lorcan's hands; Ruadan had half swords and so did Patrick.

Koschei hesitated at these new threats.

I heard barking and growling. Three sleek, black wolves loped across the field and took their places: Damian, Darrius, and Drake.

Khenti, Velthur, and Zela arrived next. We formed a half circle—and I could see that Koschei was recalculating his odds.

I focused on the zombies. I raised my hands and shouted a spell. Blue light arced from my palms to the zombies. They stopped wandering the field and formed a tight circle around us.

People still fought outside the barrier, but I knew the real fight, the one that mattered most, would happen in the next few minutes.

Koschei stepped behind his minions. Then, he obviously gave them an attack order.

The first row of idiots charged us, some held weapons, but most had nothing but their Family powers.

Fire shot out from the hands of two vampires. Velthur stomped the ground and it split. Water showered upward. He drew it into his hands and tossed it at the fire-wielders.

Lorcan, Patrick, and Ruadan were quick and clever with their swords. Heads were severed and bodies collapsed into ashy piles.

The lycanthropes went for the throats, knocking down those vampires without the wits to run.

"Hey!" called Jessica as she flew over my zombie barrier. "Did I miss the fun?"

Velthur

Translated from the Memoirs of Ruadan

Velthur's people lived and died on the land that became Italy; they were the ancestors of the Rasenna, more commonly known as the Etruscans.

He was a simple farmer who lived alone. He'd always had the ability to manipulate liquids and used his gifts to find water, even in droughts, for his own crops. Other farmers were jealous and mistakenly believed it was his land that held the key to his success.

I befriended him and after a while, he guessed my true nature. He was not afraid of me, and in fact, he offered himself as a meal every now and again.

Here, I had found my sixth vampire.

Velthur accepted my offer. Other than Koschei, Velthur was the only one I hadn't Turned under duress. He liked the idea of immortality, and that he would be able to make others who would also have his gift.

He sold his farm and traveled with me.

We seven became the Ancients: the leaders of seven Families who inherited our special gifts. Because of my grandmother's prophecy, I knew we would rule for a long time.

But not forever.

Chapter 22

Jessica landed next to Patrick, and dispatched the creep he was trying to disembowel. They grinned at each other and charged forward.

I kept my gaze on Koschei, who was throwing his followers at us without putting himself in jeopardy. What an asshole. Eventually, he'd run out of vampires. But maybe that was the point.

No one approached me. I'd like to think it was because they were terrified. More likely, they'd been told that Koschei would deal with me.

Honestly, I was feeling left out.

I rose into the air and flew over the fighting

vampires. Koschei saw me coming, but what could he do? I landed in front of him.

Gabriel skidded next to me, baring his teeth and growling.

"You won't win," said Koschei.

"Yeah. I will." I cocked my fist and punched Koschei in the jaw. He flew across the field and skidded on the grass.

Koschei didn't stay down for long. He got to his feet and dusted off his clothes. Then, he zipped toward me, his fangs bared. Gabriel snarled as he dove in front of me, effectively heading off the Ancient.

Koschei used his glamour to draw fighting companions. A big vampire male went after Gabriel. Two female vampires jumped in front of their Master. They each held wicked-sharp swords.

With a wave of my hand, I made the swords fly out of their grips. Then I created two fireballs and lobbed them at the vampires.

The flames consumed them instantly.

Gabriel dispatched the vampire and returned to me, his mouth bloody and his fur matted with mud.

We advanced on Koschei.

His confidence was flagging. I couldn't kill him. I wanted to, though. Badly.

Gabriel's bark seemed to acknowledge that he wanted the Ancient's death, too.

Koschei wore a slim, silver chain. I called forth Zela's metallurgy. The necklace tightened against his pale flesh. His eyes widened and he clawed at his throat.

He might not breathe, but being choked was no fun. I resisted the urge to throw a fireball at him. Instead, I landed nimbly in front of him.

Minions crowded around Koschei, trying to protect him. I reached into their minds and told them to walk away. I told them not to listen to Koschei.

They left and kept going, even when it was obvious their Master was trying to call them back.

I faced Koschei. Ruadan appeared on his left, Velthur on his right, and Zela behind him.

"No!" Koschei's eyes were wide, panicked. "You would give up to her your right to rule? She's a Turn-blood!"

"And a beautician," I said.

I looked down at Gabriel. His gaze locked with mine, and I knew it was time. I touched Gabriel's furry head. Magic flowed from both of us and covered the man in a gold glow. Velthur, Ruadan, and Zela stepped back. It was symbolic, what they did . . . the old guard relinquishing their power.

Like it or not, I was the new ruler.

"I ban you, Koschei the Ancient. Go into the world-between-worlds."

He tried to run, tried to reach out for Ruadan, but in the end, he couldn't escape his fate. Just as I couldn't escape mine.

His gaze latched on to mine and in those empty eyes, I saw *droch fola*. He was soulless, but he was not without hatred. He faded from sight.

I knelt next to Gabriel and hugged him. He licked my face and barked joyously.

"Sit!" I commanded the zombies.

They all sat.

"Koschei has been banned," I shouted, amplifying my voice with my new glamour power. "The fighting is over!"

Koschei's minions and supporters fled. Consortium members gave chase, but it didn't matter to me if they were caught or not. The biggest threat Broken Heart had faced was gone. Forever.

I had forgotten about Lia.

She and her dragon roared out of the sky. She lobbed the fireball straight at me. I saw Gabriel try to intercept it, but with one flick of my wrist, my energy pushed him back.

It was all I had time to do.

The fireball engulfed me.

Oh, big whoop. I stepped out of the flames. The magic of my fairy dress certainly helped protect me, but I also had Lia's power, which made me less vulnerable to fire.

She was already flying away on her dragon, but she'd seen me step from the fire unscathed.

I pointed to the ground and water sprang forth to douse the burning grass.

Gabriel launched himself at me and I was flung to the ground. He barked and growled, then licked my face.

"Okay, okay!" I laughed. "Jeez!"

I stood again, and looked at the three Ancients.

One by one, they bent down on one knee and inclined their heads. The three royal princes of the lycanthropes joined them, lying on their bellies with their heads lowered.

I looked around and saw that everyone else— even Jessica—was kneeling.

Well, now.

I guess that makes me queen, doesn't it?

I woke up in a twin-sized bed with Gabriel nearly crushing the life out of me. "Hey!"

"Scooch over," he said sleepily.

I did. We had almost no space between us, but that was okay. "How do you feel?" I asked.

He grinned, that gold gaze aglow with the kind of fire I didn't want to put out.

"The shelter accommodations suck," I said. "I want to go back to the cave."

"Okay. But there is the question of what to do with the bodies sitting in the field next to the compound."

"Oh, crap. We'll have to march them back to their graves."

"Indeed." He kissed me.

And everything was all right with the world.

I took a shower and changed clothes before I tracked down Wilson.

He was staying in a large room with the other kids. Bunk beds lined the walls. Some kids were watching television, others were reading, and Brian—Jess' oldest—was playing his PSP.

Wilson was reading *Goodnight Moon* to Ralph's toddlers while Ralph watched. I stood in the doorway and listened. My heart squeezed. It was sweet watching my son be so nice to two little ones.

When Wil was done with the story, he tucked in the boys. Then he walked to a nearby bunk and sat down on the bottom bed. He looked tired and worried.

"Hi, Wilson," I said. I sat on the end of the bed, hoping he wouldn't shut me out again.

"Mom," he said. His voice broke and he put his arms around me. I held him while he wept and I got the sniffles, too, thanking God that he was okay, that we were together again.

Sniffling, he raised his head, his eyes red and snot running out his nose. He solved that problem by wiping his nose on the sleeve of his shirt.

"Honey, haven't I told you not to do that?"

He laughed. "I'll try to remember." He looked away, then back at me. "I love you, Mom. I know I've been a jerk."

"Yeah. Me, too." I brushed his hair away from his face. "I love you, honey. Nothing will ever change that."

He hadn't quite let go of me. It had been such a long time since we'd hugged or shared a laugh. I missed him, and the way he used to be. The way *we* used to be.

"Are you really married to that guy?" he asked.

"Yes," I said carefully. "He's a good guy. I . . . like him."

"Just like, huh?" He waggled his brows and I grinned.

"Okay. Maybe more than like."

"Well, he likes you, too. I can tell."

"Oh, really? How?"

"By the way he looks at you." Wilson cut his eyes toward the doorway. "He's watching you right now."

I looked over my shoulder. There was Gabriel, waiting patiently, smiling as he watched us.

He had saved my life again. Maybe in a way he hadn't realized yet.

"Do you want to say hi?"

Wilson looked at Gabriel. "Hey."

Gabriel nodded. "Hey."

I rolled my eyes. Men.

Wilson looked troubled again. "I got problems, Mom. I need help."

"I know, baby. We'll find the answers. Together."

He hugged me again.

Gabriel walked me down the hall to my room, which was a single. It was like a hotel suite, plain white with basic amenities, but I was just grateful to have a bed to sleep in.

Gabriel smiled at me and brushed his lips across mine. Yummy. If I had a working heart, it would be trying to beat out of my chest.

I sat on my bed and Gabriel sat next to me. He took my hand. "You are my life mate."

"Are you sure?" I asked. "I mean, look at me.

I'm a beautician with a high school education, I have a kid with a drug problem, and I carry a whole lot of emotional baggage."

"That is not how I see you."

"Would you have me if not for the prophecy?"

"Yes, damn it!" He looked at me, really looked at me, as though he was trying to see my soul. "Maybe you're just trying to find a reason not to be with me."

I pressed my hands together, my mind whirling. If not for the whole prophecy thing, Gabriel would've never met me. We wouldn't be together at all.

And he wouldn't have met his true life mate. Me.

"What about that whole thing where we're supposed to save the werewolves? Not only am I undead, I'm missing the parts necessary to have children."

"We've trusted the prophecy so far," he said. "Maybe we need to have faith a little longer."

Gabriel kissed me hard. I responded because . . . okay, I admit it. I loved him.

Chapter 23

I couldn't avoid cleaning up the zombie mess. Wilson went out with me. He looked around at the zombies, who were sitting right where I left them, moaning and wiggling their arms. Some were singed, others were in pieces, and we found a number of spots that were just ash.

Being away from Gabriel was making me sick again.

"Jeez, Mom!" Wilson was holding his nose. The stench was powerful. After all, the bodies had been sitting in the sun all day. Roasting. Yuck.

Luckily, we had a few volunteers who didn't

mind picking up body parts or guiding mind-less zombies around obstacles. It took half the night to get the dead into their graves (and quite honestly, I had no idea which body went where) and reburied.

I don't think I'll be calling up a zombie army again any time soon.

Wilson and I returned to the compound. We chatted the whole way. I told him about Nonna reanimating her own body, which freaked him out. I also listened to him tell me about why he smoked pot and we discussed how to get him the help he needed.

We entered the shelter (the blood lock worked for him). He looked at me, his nose wrinkling. "You smell like zombie."

I laughed. "So do you!"

He went off for a shower, and I did, too. I got dressed in more borrowed clothes. I hadn't even begun to think about where I was going to live or what I was going to do now that my home and shop were gone.

I wasn't sure how Gabriel fit into the mix. Or what would be expected of me as the new queen of the two nations. Prophecy or not, vampires and lycanthropes weren't exactly thrilled with the idea.

My nausea subsided as I went to my room,

which was how I knew Gabriel was inside even before I opened the door.

He sat on the bed looking pensive. He stood up and offered me a crystal bottle. I took it and looked at the sparkling gold liquid inside.

"What is it?"

"Something very rare. A fairy wish."

"You can bottle wishes?"

Gabriel nodded. "I kept it for a long time. Fairies that grant wishes are rare. I caught one once and saved my wish in that bottle."

"Why are you giving it to me?"

"I'm keeping my promise," he said. "It's your wish now, Patricia. You can use it to break our binding."

My heart sank to my toes. "You want to divorce me?"

"Never." Gabriel stepped close to me. "I want you to be happy."

"Gabriel," I said, making my decision. Impulsive, my ass. Sometimes, you just had to go for it and hope for the best. "You know what? I don't give a shit about the prophecy or the Ancients or anything else. I love you. I want you. Enough said. You are mine."

"And you," he said, his smile wide, "are very much mine."

I wiggled the bottle. "Are you still giving me

this wish?" I asked. "Free and clear? No backsies?"

"No backsies." He looked at me. "What do you want to do with it?"

Gabriel and I walked to the field where Johnny and Nefertiti played out their gruesome deaths.

"Johnny."

He broke free of the scene and turned his haunted eyes on me. "Patsy. Why are you here?"

"Eva looked up some information for me. Well, for you." I tugged the paper out of my pocket. "Your daughter's name is Rebecca. She's married with two grown children, one in college, the other in the army. She lives in Sacramento. She's a writer. She just finished a book called *The Life and Death of Johnny Angelo: Memoirs of My Father.*"

"She wrote a book about me?"

"Yes," I said, smiling. "Your daughter grew up knowing who you were. I think that your fiancée always loved you. One of the reasons your daughter could write that memoir is because her mother kept so much of your stuff."

He was smiling now, too. "Thank you, Patsy. Thank you."

"There's more." I looked behind him at the

frozen murder scene. Nefertiti was about to spew her pretty lies. "Your fiancée died a number of years ago. On her gravestone, one epitaph reads: 'My heart belongs to Johnny.'"

He closed his eyes, tears sliding down his cheeks. "She took it away from me." He turned back as hatred reclaimed his heart.

"Stop."

He returned to me and waited.

"If you want to be free, if you want see Elizabeth—and believe me, she's waiting for you—then you have to let go of Nefertiti. Let go of your pain."

He absorbed my words. I don't know if I got through to him or if he'd already been thinking about the horror of his own afterlife. "I'll stop. I won't let my rage keep us trapped anymore." He looked sad now. "But I still have fifty more years with her."

"Let her go. And have a little faith."

He nodded. Then he returned to the scene. He took the knife from behind his back, but instead of severing her head, he tossed it to the ground. "No more," he said. "I'm done."

Nefertiti blinked as if waking. Then she looked around. Her gaze swung to Johnny. "You bastard! You've killed us both!"

I stepped very close to the couple. Nefertiti

screamed and wailed, but I ignored her. Johnny said nothing. He'd made his choice and he was sticking by it.

I unstoppered the crystal vial. "I wish to break the binding between Johnny Angelo and Nefertiti."

A gold mist weaved out of the bottle and surrounded them. "Wish granted," said a tiny, musical voice. Then the mist was gone.

"I see Elizabeth," said Johnny. He turned to me, his expression one of happiness and gratitude. "Thank you."

"Where are you going?" cried Nefertiti. "We are bound!"

But Johnny was rising and as he did so, he faded away. She turned to me. "What have you done, witch?"

"Duh. I just broke your binding. You can thank me later."

I took Gabriel's hand and walked away.

"What now?" he said.

"Well, my sister will show up soon with her fiancé," I said. "So, we'll be planning a wedding." I raised my hand and ticked off my fingers. "We have to start a drug rehabilitation program. I have to figure out all this 'ruling two nations' stuff. And we need to find a new place to live."

"As long as I'm with you," said Gabriel, "I'm happy."

I wrapped my arms around him and kissed him.

You know what?

Being a prophecied queen ain't half bad.

Epilogue

Six weeks later . . .

Brigid was a goddess, the mother of Ruadan, and the grandmother of Patrick and Lorcan.

She was also wrong.

She peered at me, her green eyes narrowed. Strange, gold patterns pulsed all over her body. They swirled and changed into different symbols and shapes.

The symbols were her magic, which constantly changed to accommodate whatever healing spells she needed.

Dr. Stan Michaels stood on the other side of me, writing on a chart.

He was wrong, too.

"I'm dead," I reminded them.

"You have a heartbeat," he pointed out. "And you're breathing."

Those two things I had figured out for myself. I could also shape-shift into a wolf, but that was nothing compared to the news I'd just received. "I have no uterus."

"Yes, you do," countered Dr. Michaels. "I just x-rayed you twice."

Gabriel sat next to me on the examining table. He held my hand tightly.

"Don't you believe in miracles?" asked Brigid in her lyrical Irish accent. "You've been given one."

"Three, actually," said Dr. Michaels.

"Triplets," I said.

"Triplets," repeated Gabriel.

We looked at each other and grinned.

Drinking Gabriel's blood had given me the gift of heartbeats and breathing and shape-shifting. My body had been made whole again.

We were doing all right in our new leadership roles, though getting vampires and lycans to play nice wasn't all that easy.

She shall bind with the outcast, and with this union, she will save the dual-natured.

I had never imagined that the prophecy meant I would literally save the dual-natured. Whether or not they liked it, the future of vampires and werewolves was growing in my regenerated womb.

The next generation of *loup de sang*.

A LETTER FROM PATSY

Dear Sean,

I'm sorry to hear that you are in jail. I hope you are doing well. And I mean that. We had a lot of years together and while they weren't all sunshine and roses, I think I'm a better person because of our marriage.

Wilson is in a program for recovering drug addicts. He's doing really well. You should be proud of him. I go to meetings, too, and that's why I'm writing to you.

I want you to know that I forgive you. I don't know how hard it is to live with the demons that drive you. Or what it's like to crave alcohol so badly you'd do anything to get it. Whatever you did, whatever you said, it's okay. I'm at peace with our past.

I hope that you can forgive me, too. I wasn't

the easiest person to please or to live with. I know my flaws could drive a saint to distraction. All the same, I don't think we would've made it. It took me eighteen years to realize we weren't meant to be.

Now I know what it's like to be with your soul mate. It's not all sunshine and roses, either (ha, ha), but it doesn't matter, because love always smooths out the bumps in the road.

You don't have to write me back. But if you want to, that would be just fine.

I wish you so much happiness, Sean. And love. Good luck to you.

Sincerely,
Patsy

THE SEVEN ANCIENTS

(In Order of Creation)

Ruadan: (Ireland) He flies and uses fairy magic.

Koschei: (Russia) He is the master of glamour and mind control.

Hua Mu Lan: (China) She is a great warrior who creates and controls fire.

Durga: (India) She calls forth, controls, and expels demons.

Velthur: (Italy) He controls all forms of liquid.

Amahté: (Egypt) He talks to spirits, raises the dead, creates zombies, and reinserts souls into dead bodies.

Zela: (Nubia) She manipulates all metallic substances.

GLOSSARY

A ghrá mo chroi: (Irish Gaelic) love of my heart

A stóirín: (Irish Gaelic) my little darling

A Thaisce: (Irish Gaelic) my dear/darling/treasure

Cac capaill: (Irish Gaelic) horseshit

Damnú air: (Irish Gaelic) damn it

Deamhan fola: (Irish Gaelic) blood devil

Draba: (Romany) spell/charm

Droch fola: (Irish Gaelic) bad or evil blood

Gadjikane: (Romany) non-Gypsy

Filí: (Old Irish) poet-Druid

Ja: (German) yes

Glossary

Liebling: (German) darling

Loup de Sang: (French) blood wolf

Mo chroi: (Irish Gaelic) my heart

Muló: (Romany) living dead

Roma: (Romany) member of a nomadic people originating in Northern India or Gypsies considered as a group

Romany/Romani: (Romany) language of the Roma

Solas: (Irish Gaelic) light

Sonuachar: (Irish Gaelic) soul mate

Strigoi mort: (Romany) vampire

Vampire Terms

Revised and Updated by Lorcan O'Halloran

Ancient: Refers to one of the original seven vampires. The very first vampire was Ruadan, the biological father of Patrick and Lorcan. Several centuries ago, Ruadan and his sons took the last name of "O'Halloran," which means "stranger from overseas."

Banning: (see entry: World-Between-Worlds)

Glossary

Any vampire can be sent into limbo, but the spell must be cast by an Ancient or, in a few cases, their offspring. A vampire cannot be released from banning until they feel true remorse for their evil acts. This happens rarely, which means banning is not done lightly.

The Binding: When vampires have consummation sex (with any living person or creature), they're bound together for a hundred years. This was Ruadan I's brilliant idea to keep vamps from sexual intercourse while blood-taking. No one's ever broken a binding.

The Consortium: About five hundred years ago, Patrick and Lorcan created the Consortium to figure out ways that paranormal folks could make the world a better place for all beings. Many sudden leaps in human medicine and technology are because of the Consortium's work.

Donors: Mortals who serve as sustenance for vampires. The Consortium screens and hires humans to be food sources. Donors are paid well and given living quarters. Not all vampires follow the guidelines created by the Consortium for feeding. A mortal may have been a donor without ever realizing it.

Drone: Mortals who do the bidding of their

vampire Masters. The most famous was Igor, drone to Dracula. The Consortium's Code of Ethics forbids the use of drones, but plenty of vampires still use them.

Family: Every vampire can be traced to one of the seven Ancients. The Ancients are divided into the Seven Sacred Sects, also known as the Families.

Gone to Ground: When vampires secure places where they can lie undisturbed for centuries, they "go to ground." Usually they let someone know where they are located, but we don't know the resting locations of many vampires.

Lycanthropes: Also called lycans. These shape-shifters can shift from a human into a wolf. Lycans have been around a long time and originate in Germany. They worship the lunar goddess. Their numbers are small because they don't have many females, and most children born have a fifty percent chance of living to the age of one.

Master: The vampire who successfully Turns a human is the new vamp's protector. Basically, a Master is supposed to show the Turn-blood how to survive as a vampire, unless another Master agrees to take over the education. A Turn-blood has the protection of the Family (see: Family or

Seven Sacred Sects) to which their Master belongs.

Roma: The Roma are cousins to full-blooded lycanthropes. They can change only on the night of the full moon. Just as full-blooded lycanthropes are raised to protect vampires, the Roma are raised to hunt vampires.

Seven Sacred Sects: The vampire tree has seven branches. Each branch is called a Family and each Family is directly traced to one of the seven Ancients. The older you are, the more mojo you get. A vampire's powers are related to his Family.

Taint: The black plague for vampires. Thanks to experiments with Lorcan's unusual blood, Consortium scientists have formulated a cure for the disease.

Turn-blood: A human who's been recently Turned into a vampire. If you're less than a century old, you're a Turn-blood.

Turning: Vampires can't have babies. They perpetuate the species by Turning humans. Unfortunately, only one in about ten humans actually makes the transition.

World-Between-Worlds: The place between this

plane and the next where there is a void. Some people can slip back and forth between this "veil."

Wraiths: Rogue vampires who believed they were at the top of the food chain. After the defeat of their leader, Ron, aka Ragnvaldr, it appeared they had been disbanded. However, the Ancient Koschei was the true leader and he took up the banner of vampire domination.

NOTE FROM THE AUTHOR

My research took me to ancient Egypt, one of my all-time favorite places. Do you know how many times I've watched *The Mummy* and *The Mummy Returns*? Okay, not exactly research, but I've watched numerous documentaries, bought many research books (and they're big and heavy, too), and I even have a small collection of cool Egyptian knickknacks. Nothing actually from ancient Egypt, but all the same, they're really cool.

I tried to make the Turning of my vampires somewhat interesting. I know that Patrick Turned Lorcan, but let's just say after Lor killed him, Ruadan came along and did all the mumbo jumbo to make his other son a vampire. So I have written it, so it will be. Ta-da!

You may have noticed the emphasis on alcoholism in this novel. This is not a subject I had to research since I've lived with alcoholics all my life. Some people are ashamed about what goes on in their homes. They're afraid to get help or afraid of what others might think about them.

Let me tell you something: You deserve safety, good health, and happiness. Help is available 24/7. You just have to decide to ask for it. Pick up a phone, get on the Internet, or walk to a friend's house.

I highly recommend this Web site for anyone who is affected by alcoholism: http://www.al-anon.alateen.org.

You are not alone. You deserve love. You are worthy of a better life.

And baby, that's the truth.

Keep reading for a sneak peek of the
next novel in Michele Bardsley's
Broken Heart paranormal series,

Wait Till Your
Vampire Gets Home

Coming from Signet Eclipse
in November 2008

I hugged the large oak tree as I tried to catch my breath. Sneaking around this creepy little town in the dark—and during winter, no less— was not one of my better ideas. Especially after I'd been scared out of my wits by those . . . those *howls*.

Shivers raced up and down my spine. What in the world had made those terrifying sounds? Surely not dogs. Coyotes? Wolves? Eek! My shivering turned into full-body shudders. My parents were convinced that real werewolves roamed the woods. They'd spent their whole lives trying to prove that paranormal beings, aliens, other dimensions, and all kinds of weird and wacky things existed.

Despite never finding a single speck of evidence, my parents still believed in all that hooha. As soon as I hit eighteen, I checked out of their world of insanity and entered wonderful, sensible, logical reality.

I listened for the howls, relieved when I heard nothing but the wind rattling the branches above me. Some reporter I was! Hadn't I come here on the trail of an arsonist? I wasn't supposed to let little things like rabid dogs (ack!) and bad weather stop me from getting the story. This was my chance to prove I was made of sterner stuff. I had to find this guy before anyone else, so I could ditch my piddling assignments. If I had to write one more obituary . . . argh!

I pressed my cheek against the tree. No warmth there. Why hadn't I thought of a ski mask? The black parka had done a fair job of keeping most of me warm, but the hood offered no protection to my face. My skin felt scraped raw by the freezing air. And the rough bark wasn't exactly helping, either.

I let go of the tree, but stayed close. Okay. I needed to regroup. I let my thoughts drift around the information I'd accumulated so far.

The arsonist was nicknamed Dragon. He always started fires on the roofs of buildings. He never used an accelerant, so the police couldn't figure out how he started such hot, fast fires. My contact in the police department said that detectives believed that Dragon was from Broken Heart.

I readjusted the strap of my purse, which clunked in protest. I was a big believer in being prepared. My parents might be a taco short of a combination platter, but they'd taught me many skills. MacGyver had nothing on me.

I inhaled, but didn't really appreciate the loamy smell of earth and the crisp scent of pine—mostly because it felt like tiny icicles were forming in my nose and my lungs.

I'd forgotten my gloves, but though my hands were Popsicles, I clenched the oak. Heart pounding, I peered around the wide trunk.

A man was burying a coffin.

It looked new, though the grave was not. The heart-shaped marble tombstone looked worse for wear; the top right corner had broken off.

Oh, this was *much* better than running away from the scary clamor of unknown creatures.

I was fairly close, but because my glasses were flotsam in the junk sea of my purse, I had to squint to read the inscription:

THERESE ROSEMARIE GENESSA
BELOVED WIFE AND MOTHER
1975—2005

How he managed to maneuver the mahogany casket into the hole, I don't know. He was strong, even though he looked like a normal guy. Nice bod, but not one made by Bowflex. It was his apparent normalcy that perplexed me. Hmm. What kind of person buried a casket at nearly ten at night? Hey! What if he was a drug dealer or a gunrunner hiding the goods?

My excitement drained almost immediately. Neither of those scenarios felt right. He wasn't trying to be covert. And wouldn't someone burying something other than a body have a second guy watching? Or at least look over his shoulder more often?

The sad truth was that I had probably stumbled upon an employee of the cemetery.

Well, poop.

The silence was ungodly. No chirping of crickets, stirring of little animals, or twittering of birds. In this odd quiet, the shovel rasped unpleasantly as the man thrust it into the pile of dark soil and tossed it into the grave. The earth thudded onto the coffin.

Rasp. *Thud.* Rasp. *Thud.*

I studied the rest of the cemetery. Nearly all the graves had fresh dirt on them. Their tombstones were tilted, broken, or fallen. The place looked as if it had been ravaged by an earthquake. Seismic activity in Oklahoma? Not exactly the scintillating news I was hoping for—although it would be a change from tornadoes.

My gaze returned to the man. It seemed wrong to get any closer. After all, he was completing an awful task. But I was curious. I also wasn't interested in retracing my steps. I might accidentally find the source of those hair-raising howls. He might not know it, but he was the closest thing to safety I had right now.

About five feet away was a lone pine tree with thickly covered branches. I shot out from my cover and raced to the pine, ducking under its flagging limbs. The needles poked at me, so I scrunched down and watched him. I was near enough to see his determined expression. He had brown hair, cut short. A nice, friendly face. Not drop-dead gorgeous, but pleasant.

I crouched next to the tree and froze my butt off while watching him fill up the entire hole. I don't know why I stayed. Watching a man do this heart-wrenching work wasn't exactly chasing down the big story. I guess I just didn't want to leave. I felt like someone needed to be there standing watch with him, even if he was un-aware of my presence. Stupid, right?

You're too soft, Libs. That's why you'll never get far in this biz. Hah! What did my editor-in-chief know? He was jaded. Wearied by the job. Due for retirement. I'd gotten my degree in journalism because I wanted to find real news about real people. Squishing down people's major life moments into twenty-five words or less was still better than slogging through the Louisiana swamps looking for Bayou Boo, half man and half alligator.

Yikes! It was so cold! I clamped my lips together to keep my teeth from chattering. The man patted down the dirt with the flat end of the shovel. He wore a light jacket, jeans, and sneakers, not exactly cold-weather gear. Yet he didn't seem all that affected by the freezing temperatures.

He stared at the grave and I stared at him. Something about him niggled at me. His face was a shade too pale. I couldn't fault a guy who wasn't into baking his skin. No, it was his utter stillness that freaked me out.

Then I realized he wasn't sweating. Not a drop. After lifting a coffin and then burying it, he wasn't perspiring. He wasn't even out of breath.

"You can come out now." He leaned on the shovel and turned his gaze directly to the pine tree. To *me*.

How had I given myself away? Even though moments earlier I'd thought of him as my safety net, I wasn't going to stroll out and introduce myself. He was good at digging graves; I didn't want to be the next one he buried.

"You are not afraid. You will come to me," he said. His voice dropped an octave and went all seductive. A grave digger who wanted to put the moves on the lurking stranger. In a cemetery. Yuck.

I clutched the tree while my mind raced. Oh, to hell with it. I ducked out from underneath the unwieldy branches and raced toward the forest.

I heard the growls two seconds before I saw the animals issuing the threats. Two huge, pissed-off wolves loped toward me.

Ohmygodohmygodohmygod!

"Aaaaaaaaahhhh!" My scream echoed into the dense forest. Heart thumping, stomach roiling, fear prickling, I made a U-turn and ran back the other way. Their growls gave way to fierce barking.

REPORTER EATEN BY KILLER CANINES. That would be the headline. My boss would tell everyone at my funeral, *I told Libby she didn't have the chops for*

301

the job, but I never thought she'd end up as chops.
And he'd guffaw, that evil bastard. I was so putting salt in his sugar dispenser when I got back to the office.

I shot past the pine tree. He was still there! My grave-digging safety man! His puzzled expression switched to alarm. His eyes went wide and he dropped the shovel, which was a good thing, because I launched myself at him.

He caught me, staggered backward, and then tried to let me go.

"Pick me up! Pick me up!" I screeched. "Save me already!"

ABOUT THE AUTHOR

Award-winning, national bestselling author **Michele Bardsley** lives in Oklahoma with her family. She escapes the drudgery of housework by writing stories about vampire moms, demon hunters, interfering goddesses, cursed wizards, and numerous other characters living in worlds of magic and mayhem. She loves to hear from her fans! Visit her Web site at www.MicheleBardsley.com or drop by the Broken Heart Web site at www.BrokenHeartOK.com.

I'M THE VAMPIRE, THAT'S WHY
by Michele Bardsley

Does drinking blood make me a bad mother?

Broken Heart is the city with the highest rate of divorce and highest percentage of single parents in Oklahoma. And I, Jessica Matthews, have been a member of that club ever since my husband dumped me for his twentysomething secretary and then had the gall to die in a car accident.

Now I'm not just a single mother trying to make ends meet in this crazy world....I'm also a vampire. One minute I was taking out the garbage; the next I awoke sucking on the thigh of superhot vampire Patrick O'Halloran, who'd generously offered his femoral artery to save me.

But though my stretch marks have disappeared and my vision has improved, I can't rest until the thing that did this to me is caught. My kids' future is at stake... figuratively and literally. As is my sex life. Although I wouldn't mind finding myself attached to Patrick's juicy thigh again, I learned that once a vampire does the dirty deed, it hitches her to the object of her affection for at least one hundred years. I just don't know if I'm ready for that kind of commitment....

Don't Talk Back to Your Vampire

by Michele Bardsley

*Sometimes it's hard to take your own advice—
or pulse.*

Ever since a master vampire became possessed and
bit a bunch of parents, the town of Broken Heart,
OK, has catered to those of us who don't rise until
sunset—even if that means PTA meetings at midnight.

As for me, Eva LeRoy, town librarian and single
mother to a teenage daughter, I'm pretty much used
to being "vampified." You can't beat the great side
effects: no crow's-feet or cellulite! But books still
make my undead heart beat—and, strangely enough,
so does Lorcán the Loner. My mama always told me
everyone deserves a second chance. Still, it's one
thing to deal with the usual undead hassles: rival
vamps, rambunctious kids adjusting to night school,
and my daughter's new boyfriend, who's a vampire
hunter, for heaven's sake. It's quite another to fall for
the vampire who killed you....

"The paranormal romance of the year."
—MaryJanice Davidson

"Hot, hilarious, one helluva ride."
—L. A. Banks